Essence *of a*
Dragon

By

S J Ward

Grosvenor House
Publishing Limited

This book is published by
Grosvenor House Publishing Ltd
Link House
140 The Broadway, Tolworth, Surrey, KT6 7HT.
www.grosvenorhousepublishing.co.uk

This book is a work of fiction. Any resemblance to
people or events, past or present, is purely coincidental.

A CIP record for this book
is available from the British Library

ISBN 978-1-83975-930-7

For my wife and daughter,
Julie and Louise.
You really had to put up with a lot.

Acknowledgments

Where do you start? I suppose with the places that are real within this novel. Therefore I will start in chronological order.

My thanks must go to Lynn and Iain Brown at Invercoe Highland Holidays. To Ed Daynes at the Clachaig Inn. To Kirsty Laird on behalf of the Ballachulish Hotel. To Peter Gibson on behalf of Crerar Hotels and The Gathering. To David Cooper at Crafts & Things, Glencoe. I asked these people for permission and they allowed me to continue using their locations. I hope I have done your establishments justice.

My own family, Julie and Louise, put up with a lot and continued to encourage me, thank you. And certain friends who read the early drafts and provided feedback, Kay Poole, Louise Sykes and Dorothy Bruce. I hope your task wasn't too arduous. And finally to Gary James who advised me on the very last chapter. Thank you.

The beithir is a 'real' Ballachulish legend. Sources are from... Superstitions of the Highlands and Islands of Scotland by John Gregorson Campbell Published by James MacLehose and sons in 1900.

Folk Tales and FairyLore in Gaelic and English collected by oral tradition by Rev James MacDougall, edited by Rev George Calder BD and published by John Grant of Edinburgh in 1910. An Encyclopedia of Fairies by Katherine Briggs published by Pantheon Books in 1976.

The film references speak for themselves.

The story of James Stewart and that of the Glencoe Massacre were related to me on one of my first visits to the area. Whoever told me about them at that time, thank you.

Apparently, the way my brain works, these references may be incorrectly remembered. But that's human nature for you.

Introduction

You go on holiday to relax, to get away from your regular life. Sometimes there are people to visit or things that need doing while you're away. But basically, it's a change of scenery, doing something you enjoy. You certainly do not expect to be caught up in the outrageously weird events that befall Miles. Events that affect the people he has placed around him, innocent friends and his wife, who are drawn, eventually, into everything that happens to him. True friends.

Miles's dragon initiates that!

Chapter 1

Miles and Julie left their motorhome, both of them clad in dry waterproof coats and leggings and each wearing sturdy walking boots. The leaden clouds above promised a drear, dank day; dreich, they'd call it here.

Between them, they were toting only a single, small, heavily-packed, rucksack, and Miles wore it on his back, strapped down tight. An angular protrusion within the bag dug into the small of his back, uncomfortable but bearable, it provided an unerring reminder of what the day was really about, what they'd come here to do. He'd continue to bear it until the time came when the sack would become substantially lighter and Julie would take her turn to carry it. In turn, that would herald the time to about-face, and head back down the glen towards their temporary home in Invercoe.

They always came up to Scotland in January, regardless of the weather. Come rain, hail, sleet or snow, they'd arrive after Hogmanay and return home before Burns night. This year, it seemed, was the turn of rain to coincide with their holiday, a holiday that was their most important one of the year, the one they enjoyed the most, and today, the time spent here held an added poignancy.

Miles Better, sixty years old now, generally, didn't look his age. He probably could have appeared ten years younger if he had shaved that morning or had had a haircut, but things like that just didn't seem important today. His mousy-coloured, full head of hair hadn't even been combed through, and the almost white stubble on his chin just helped to exaggerate his stern, crease-marked face. A face full of quality, each line told the story of a hard-worked life in the outdoors, a face like the cracked leather on a well worn boot, features that had lived with and battled the elements. Under the sun his hair would almost turn blonde and he'd tan well; something to do with his parentage, his mother was born and bred in Hong Kong, Miles's father, British through and through, met her when he was stationed there after the war. But they were both long gone now, a part of history that Miles would often contemplate. 'Would they be proud of what their son had become?'

Miles prided himself on being slim and athletic in build, never having to go to a gym to hone muscles or to work-out on removing excess droopy bits, those superfluous, dangly, jowls that a lot of his friends seemed to sport. The overall package would normally cause any one who met him to comment on how well he looked. Today though, he didn't look well, more pallid than usual, scruffy in appearance, and his face set with a rigour-hardened grimace. Still, he was gentlemanly and gentle and he held onto Julie's hand, his wife of thirty-seven years, as they walked away from the campsite in Invercoe.

Following the road towards Glencoe, with hoods up and heads bowed slightly, to prevent a soaking from the rain that now stair-rodded vertically, they plodded on, hand in hand, Julie on the side away from the road because Miles *always* walked on the road side of the path. They crossed over to the opposite side before the main-road junction, Miles unconsciously skirting around Julie to take her other hand and remain between her and any traffic. They made their way into Glencoe village, heading towards the war memorial and the footpath up the glen. It was eerily quiet, everyone with any sense, if they weren't at work, would not be venturing out in this weather. The continuous, muffled, pitter-patter of raindrops upon their Goretex hoods were as audibly, all-consuming, as a jackhammer at twenty paces, and stilted any attempt at conversation between them.

Once on the path through the woodland, and away from the road, but still following the road's trend upwards through the glen, they both pulled down their hoods and stopped for a breather. Sheltered for a while from the rain, by the tall coniferous trees that bound the path, Miles removed a tin from his pocket and opened it up to fiddle out a dry, pre-rolled, cigarette, careful not to soak it with his wet hands, holding it with only the very tips of a thumb and forefinger before placing it carefully between his lips. Fumbling into the pocket again, he found his lighter, and, after numerous attempts thumbing the striker-wheel of the increasingly sodden device, lit up. He inhaled deeply, then in a single, long, slow stream, he exhaled the smoke that had hit its mark. Frowning, he looked about furtively, behind and ahead on the pathway, there was nothing! Julie, noticing Miles's action, stepped towards him, and held out her hand to hold his.

'Are you okay, love?' she asked quietly and with concern. Miles just nodded a slight affirmative reply.

In return, she replied, voicelessly, by gently squeezing his hand a little more tightly before releasing it; a minute gesture, that spoke more than words could say.

She was always on the ball when it came to emotions, especially Miles's. She had an ability to spot even the tiniest sign that something, maybe, wasn't right or that single second when his hand needed holding. It infuriated Miles at times, but not today. Miles had always considered himself to be the practical sort, the provider of the house, putting money in the bank, food on the table and, most importantly, he was Julie's protector. It was down to Miles to be on hand to handle every situation and to keep emotional reactions to a minimum; Miles should have the answers, and to be able to deal with everything that was thrown at him. Even physically, in their life together, Miles's hand would always be over Julie's and to the front of her delicate hand, shielding her, leading her and loving her. It was borne of up-bringing, it was natural, and the way it was meant to be. Like a mother leading a child, showing that same love, devotion and protection. Miles had been trained by his own mother, without even realising that a lesson was in session, and it had stayed with him. Once upon a time he had been led and protected, then, as he grew older he took on the responsibilities of a man, and now he did the protecting.

Julie stood back a little from Miles, and looked anxiously upon him as he smoked. She was definitely keeping things together better than Miles, it was as if she were just waiting for the moment when his outward show of solidity collapsed like a house of cards, the second when that impassive facade crumbled and tumbled to the floor, shattering into a million shards, and she knew, *she,* would be there to help pick up the pieces, and put everything back into its proper place.

Slightly younger than Miles, slightly slighter, Julie Better lived with an attitude of 'take me the way you find me'. It wasn't laziness, but she never felt the need to doll herself up, or smother her face in make-up and be a girlies girl, she was more than happy to wear practical clothing; attire that suited her lifestyle. Flat sensible shoes, often walking boots, instead of high heels; trousers, very rarely dresses or skirts; blouses were for weddings and funerals, and sweaters were for warmth. Her hair she kept short and tidy and its non-uniform, pewter and silver, sullied by her original brunette colour was testament to it sporting no hair colourant products whatsoever, it was naturally that mixture, right down to the roots. When Miles joked that it was salt and pepper but the pepper was running out, Julie didn't care, she would get her own back on Miles later that week, somehow, hopefully when he least expected it. In the meantime, she'd just smile and await her turn to have a dig at Miles in retaliation. Julie had smooth, pale skin that contrasted greatly with Miles's and in the summer they'd compare the depths of their tans, arm against arm, his and hers. Julie's would display only the slightest of a bleached, beech, honeyed tan, whereas Miles's arm would take on the appearance of a dark, English oak, barley-twist table leg.

Even though they seemed in total contrast to one another, chalk and cheese, they complimented each other, they were two sides of the same coin and you could never have one without the other.

'Come on, lets get moving again.' Miles said with summoned authority before taking one last, fleetingly expectant, look the way they'd come and heading off along the path again. 'Let me know if I'm going too fast!'

Julie fell in behind him like a trained puppy and followed, she knew she wouldn't struggle to keep up with him, Miles also knew that, but he'd politely ask at odd times along the way. Steadily they made their way up the glen towards the first target of the day and lunch.

The Clachaig Inn provided the welcomed stop-off for lunch, and at this time of year they were assured a seat by one of the fires, and a chance to dry their sodden outer layers. Miles removed the rucksack and placed it down reverently, by the side of the table. They both removed their coats and waterproof leggings, placing them on the backs of the chairs, nearest the hearth, to steam rigidly dry. Miles left Julie and approached the long bar to order drinks and get the menu. The bar hadn't changed much, behind the counter and against the back wall, bottles of whisky sat in ranks and rows, a whole wall of whisky set out from 'A to Z', from left to right; not that Miles could think of a whisky that began with a 'Z'.

On a previous visit, Miles had set out on his attempt, to drink a tot from every bottle placed along that wall, starting at 'A' and seeing where it led, by the end of that evening he had reached the letter 'C', or was it somewhere in the 'B's; After one too many whisky's, Miles had become somewhat confused. Ordering large whisky's, possibly, wasn't the best way of achieving a personal record either. Hadn't he already had a double Bowmore?

Nowadays his selections were from a tried and tested batch, the excesses of his youth now replaced by the sensibilities of age. He ordered a large Bunnahabhain for himself, and a gin and tonic for Julie, made mental note of the specials on the menu board and returned to sit opposite her to relay the details.

In the middle of the table in front of them, sat the most important of the contents from the rucksack, Julie had removed it and placed it there; centre-table like an ornament.

The pine box, nine inches by three by three, was surmounted by a small brass plaque with four letters etched into it, they spelt the name 'Skip'. Miles slid the gin and tonic across the table and into Julie's waiting hand, picking up his own glass he raised it in a toast, Julie followed Miles's suit, and raised her own glass, both glasses now hovered above the box, almost touching, Miles's glass trembling in the air minutely.

In a broken, barely audible, voice Miles said 'To Skip.' the two glasses touched momentarily with a subtle, muted 'clink', Julie took a dainty sip from her glass and Miles knocked back the entire contents of his.

Once again that day, Julie reached across to hold Miles's hand, tightening her grip fractionally, as she noticed the early signs of moisture welling up in the corners of his eyes. Miles attempted to take another sip of his whisky from his now empty glass and upon realising its lack of content, pulled his hand away from Julie's, to cradle the glass with both hands, leaving greasy impressions of his thumb and fingerprints on the outside of the glass. He sat back and turned his head to face away from her, desperately trying to compose himself. Julie stood up and wandered over to the bar to fetch him another dram, slightly disappointed in that Miles wouldn't allow her to help him.

Both of them opted to have soup for lunch, neither feeling that they had an appetite for a main course, they would have a main dinner later that evening back at the motorhome. Miles disappeared outside for a while to have a quick cigarette before their fare arrived, and when he returned he purchased two more drinks from the bar. On retaking his seat, he raised his glass once more towards Julie. Julie looked him in the eyes and noted that, although they were reddened, he'd wiped away any sign of tears from them. He delivered a more restrained toast this time, even though it was more emotionally charged, his voice didn't quaver, it was as if he'd been rehearsing outside.

'Skip's last visit to his favourite place, and to you, love! Thank you!' They clinked glasses again and drank, relishing in the warmth radiating from the fire and immersed themselves in their own worlds for a while, until their food order was called. Sitting silently and staring into space, they'd both thought about Skip.

Skip was Miles's dog, though he be excessively protective of Julie, he always sought the protection of

Miles. A large, black and white, classic border-collie, who had been a part of their lives for twelve years. He was loyal, so loyal; not brave, a bit of a wuss really; had his moments of naughtiness, but gave *his* love to *his* master unreservedly. Being with Skip, especially here in Scotland, was always a joy. Skip would often lead the way until he knew he should wait for you, he'd always have one eye on where you were, or where you were going, he'd even find a bench to sit by, when he realised, that *you* needed to take a break for a few minutes. Unfortunately, Skip contracted bone cancer and a few months earlier, the hardest decision Miles had ever made, had to be made. Even the death of Miles's father, hadn't resulted in the amount of distress and sadness that followed the loss of Skip. Today, they would scatter Skip's ashes into the River Coe, just upstream of the Clachaig from the bridge that crossed it, where Skip would be free to run through the heather and splash through the streams eternally, and would never be forgotten; that's what Miles wanted to believe, and Miles clung to those wishes, as much as he would have clung to Skip, if only things had been different.

Outside, the rain had stopped for a while, it was time. With as cheery a farewell and thank-you as they could muster, they payed their tab, left the inn and followed the narrow road towards the bridge. Once there, Miles removed his Leatherman multi-tool from a pocket, and selected a screwdriver from within it. Julie took the rucksack and removed the box, then carefully, while Julie held the box upside down, Miles removed the six screws that held the baseplate in place on the little wooden coffin. Inside there was a plastic bag containing the grey and white ashes, grey like the day, but at least for this moment, dry.

Over the parapet of the bridge, the bag was split open with a penknife blade, and, solemnly, the contents were released into the river below them. Julie and Miles remained in silence for a number of minutes, not wanting to speak or leave, not wanting to be the first to break the trance-like state they maintained, and certainly not wanting to finally say goodbye. Their reverie was only broken by the cars, that passed within feet of them as they contemplated their loss. Looking away from the water that tumbled towards the sea, about them, as they stood there, the mountains of Glencoe sat sombrely shrouded in cloud, weeping waterfalls, as if paying their last respect.

The air was full of moisture, as they made their way back down towards Invercoe. It was colder now, and the clouds, that had previously hidden the upper slopes of the mountains, had enveloped them completely. Deep in thought, Miles led the way down, Julie in tow behind with her own thoughts.

Miles pictured in his mind the imperfect release of the ashes. He didn't feel he wanted to discuss it with Julie, the images just wound round and around and twisted in his head. Those bloody cars! They ruined it! The shitty weather! If only the ashes had been swept away by the river in one! At the small ceremonial scattering, the majority of the ashes had just sunk towards the edge of the river's flow, clumped together like leaden candy-floss; a sticky mass with only wisps of the outer coating breaking off to travel seawards. Like sick, it just remained there to blight the river bed, it should have dispersed! Some of the ashes *had* carried downstream but the majority remained right before his eyes, marring the perfect river! He couldn't even get that simple task right! He couldn't even organise a piss-up in a brewery! Miles's thoughts stabbed, seared and stung.

With every step of their descent towards home, Miles's demeanour became more and more morose. Julie watched from behind, the decline, as Miles snatched randomly at the hood of his coat in annoyance, trying to rip it free of his encumbered head, she could sense the anger that was swelling up inside of him, and she daredn't say a word or make a move to help quash the torment that was building, fortifying before her. Any attempt to subdue Miles's anger now, would only be met with a tirade of foulness, it would never diffuse the situation, boiling there in front of her. She knew when to keep quiet, and when to not even proffer a comforting hand to re-affirm the unity they usually had.

A slight breeze attempted to re-seat the hood upon Miles's head, and he flailed about wildly to remove it again, preferring becoming soaking wet in the mizzle that they walked through, rather than dry and comfortable. Miles was seeking and yearning for pain. A deserved retribution, the pain he'd experienced in the vets, the day Skip was put to sleep and removed from his life was torturous and now it was becoming amplified. It wasn't right, he'd made an ill-judged decision based upon spurious information. He'd killed Skip, as if he'd throttled the life from the dog with his own bare hands, and Miles couldn't live with that!

He didn't want to live with that! The fact that he'd just watched, helpless, as the lethal injection was given, bought on even more discomfort. Skip had trusted him, snaffled down the biscuit treats he had been offered and died in his arms, trusting that there would be more. Miles knew without any doubt he should have stopped it. Skip should still be here. Why the fuck wasn't he here?

All this while, Julie dared not speak, She wanted to laugh, to shout out at him for being such a baby, to slap him, to shock him back to her, to let him know that she was suffering too. 'It isn't all about you, Miles!' But she loved him, so instead she did, nothing!

As they approached the door of the motorhome, Julie turned her back to allow Miles to reach into the top compartment of the rucksack and locate the van keys, he passed them to her and in the last few seconds of any rationalism that Miles had left, he spat through gritted teeth...

'Im going for a walk, I'll be back later!' Harsh and final with no chance for discussion and leaving no way of dissuading him from his course.

With those venomously delivered words he was gone, accelerating rapidly away from her. Julie watched him stamp off into the encompassing gloom and spray, she felt discarded, rejected and alone but she knew Miles was better off without her for a while, and she was certainly better off without him. She was frightened but most of all, she was worried. Undoubtably, Miles would come back to her, tail between his legs, his eyes would plead for forgiveness, and maybe it would be down to her to initiate that process of forgiveness, but for now, they were better off being apart, otherwise Miles would just lock himself away and never let her in, he'd never let go of his torment. Julie unlocked the door to the motorhome and let herself into the warm interior to cry quietly, alone.

Chapter 2

The screaming and shouting, although it was all in the mind and not audible to anyone who might hear, had stopped, but the throwing was about to begin. There was an imperative need to be as destructive as possible, to vent what remained of his frustration towards a new target, an inanimate wreck on the foreshore that had been there, possibly the whole of his life and probably for other lifetimes before his. With countless weapons to select from, strewn along this scraggy shoreline; more rock than beach, more seaweed than sand; Miles sat amidst the tattered, sea-worn debris, selecting smoothed stone missiles at random, to hurl at the greasy bones of the long dead boat.

Satisfaction wasn't forthcoming. From his sitting position upon a raised, damp, mound of rock, Miles's aim was hindered and inaccurate, he was becoming incensed and unhinged. Handfuls of gravel, the new ammunition of choice, randomly scooped up, started to splatter the pools of water left by the retreating tide, skittering and clattering across the bigger stones and rocks, and ricocheting haphazardly. Those individual fragments that hit, the fossilised wooden target of his rage, gave no satisfaction or release. Larger stones too now, caused no discernible damage, but for bigger splashes if they hit a rock pool, or a louder, duller, thud, if they hit the boat's fetid timbers.

The whole exercise was futile, Miles had expected to see a scene of uttermost destruction, a forest fire out of control and raging, an inferno to rival his inner turmoil, broken bones and shattered remnants, desolation and destruction combined. Instead, he'd rearranged some stones on the beach, and even he couldn't tell which ones he'd actually moved. Instead of carnage, a slight wisp of smoke as the fires petered out and died, flames that had never got a grip on anything, withered, not even a spark now, not even the smell of cordite in the air. The wreck sat seemingly oblivious to his weak, pointless demonstration of superiority and power.

Miles didn't know how he'd arrived on the beach, he'd walked blindly, and found himself before the remains of the boat. His initial idea was to walk and walk, eternally, away from his past, walk until he collapsed with fatigue. Maybe Death would take him and he'd be happy with that, he'd embrace the cold, he just needed to escape. Inside, he just wanted to die.

Miles summoned up one more scream now, a torturous, whole-body scream from deep within, every ounce of remaining energy pushing forward his anger, though full of despair, in one final, tumultuous, vocal explosion. As the breath was gone from his body, the wail diminished like the flames, and Miles was left deflated, ashamed and lost.

There was no echo and no reverberation, the light drizzle in the air just absorbed the noise to a nothingness, a mournful, bereaved whimper like the dying of the day disappearing into the night. Miles clasped his head in his hands and sat, empty. Tears slowly formed and ran beneath his fingers, totally indistinguishable from the dampness that already coated his hands. Bits of grit indented his face as he pressed into it with both hands, trying to force away the anguish he felt, trying to replace it with a physical pain, he wanted to crush the life from his body. When at last he removed his hands from his face to stare, dejectedly, into nothingness, rivulets of water ran from his sodden hair, to wash away the grit, and dilute the tears.

'Have you quite finished?' said a voice, clearer than the day, shining out above the background sounds of the sea lapping the shoreline. The drizzle kissing the rocks, stones, slates, gravel and seaweed, a muted hiss in the background. A voice that didn't belong here!

Miles span about to look behind and around, expecting to be surprised by a face, inches from his own, the face of someone who had crept up behind him while he'd been otherwise engaged, and into the face of the owner of the voice that had spoken with such clarity. No-one was there, he'd just imagined it.

'Well, have you finished?' The quality of sound appeared to come from everywhere as if Miles were wearing headphones. Like a sharp knife it cut through the clutter of this grainy, grey day like a brilliant, magnesium, white light.

Miles sprang to his feet, with a slightly off-balance flurry that bordered on fear, fight or flight? He turned wildly through a full circle, and cast his eyes both high and low to pinpoint- well, anything! There was nothing there that wasn't there before; the sea, bland and broody; the shattered shoreline, tessellated, fragmented and desolate; the larger rocks at the head of the beach, guarding like the monolithic faces of Easter Island, and above that, the grassy scrubland that stretched back towards the main road, weighed heavy with rain and drooped in static compliance. There were no places to hide, everything was too exposed, too open to view, he was alone here, wet and bedraggled, much like the shoreline itself.

'Now I've got your attention!'

The straw that broke the camel's back and Miles fled. He didn't know where he was running to, just away, and in the straightest possible line he could manage, straight was good, it saved lives. His feet kicked up gravel and he slipped and slid on seaweed, he didn't care, he skirted round larger rock boulders, and splashed through shallow pools of retained seawater, as fast as his feet would carry him, and all in the general direction of the head of the beach and the safety of the road. Shaking with fear now, the rage he'd shook with seconds before had re-invented itself, he aimed towards the path through the rocks, that had led him onto this piece of shoreline earlier that day, skidding and sliding, shinning obstacles in his path, totally focussed, his brain latched onto only one thing; flight!

'There's really no point in running!'

It was in front of him, it was too clear, it was behind him, it was within him. Miles had never ever felt this scared before, he turned his head, still going full pelt, and again tried to find where the voice emanated from. Then he was falling, flying forwards as he tripped over an immoveable rock that he'd not seen. In an unconscious reaction, his arms came to his aid to catch the ground before his face hit it and he sprawled to a grinding halt in a hail of wet gravel, seaweed and stones. Flailing about onto his back, with not a hint of pain, Miles shot glances every which way, and concentrated his attention upon every aspect of the shoreline. The sea, dreary grey and slightly further away now was serene, wavelets tumbling slowly, licking onto the shore like exploring tongues, only to be lost in the patches of dark sand, stone and weed that littered the cut-off between land and sea. The drizzle was easing and the view he beheld was becoming more vivid as light and shadow played their part.

The sky was certainly brightening and, in the distance, shafts of light pierced the threatening clouds and brought a revitalised colour to the mountains that reached down into the sea, snow capped but still with their summits hidden from view amidst the cloud. Trees along the flanks of the hills were returning from being dark black and grey, vague shapes, to the more recognisable greens and mauves of managed forested slopes.

Drawing his vision back towards his immediate quest for the source of the voice, Miles re-focussed on the shore line and the area he'd been sat to vent his rage. The jagged-toothed bones of the boat, beached and bleached by countless years, once a workable craft that carried- who knew what? It lay discarded and allowed to rot away to become a coherent part of the moonscape scene. Undoubtably, the vast majority of it was spread about or buried, only the upper timber ribs were visible like a skeleton partially interred, some planking draped the ribs like broken skin. At high tide it would be engulfed completely, to re-emerge, glistening with saltwater and bedecked with seaweed as the tide ebbed again. Such was Miles' concentration on his surroundings his shaking had ceased as he considered the wreckage. In this place there was just him and the boat really, the only visitors, all else belonged.

'You've got it!'

Wild panic remained in check but teetered at the doorway so close to breaking in. The voice he heard was coming from himself, not through his own vocalisation, but through his thoughts. It wasn't his own voice he was listening to though, but it was a voice he could associate with, however, he couldn't place where he'd heard it before, when or even who it belonged to, it was so familiar, though so forgotten.

'At least I'm not going mad then.' Miles thought about his own words as he spoke them, comparing the sound they made to the new voice, listened at the way they sounded ever so slightly shaky and latched onto their meaning being, so very improbable. He was definitely going mad!

'No, you're not going mad, you're talking to me.'

'No, I'm talking to myself, and that's a sign of going mad. I'm the only one here, and I'm talking to voices in my head.' Miles's voice sounded broken, he heard himself in the regular way, and in the very way he'd heard himself through all of his sixty years, through his ears as waves of varying pressure generated, originally, by his own vocal cords, somehow turned into electrical signals, and somehow translated by his brain into- his sound, with his meaning, something he could react upon or understand.

The new voice, the one inside his head, wasn't even like his thoughts. His thoughts could put voices there, to the memory part of the mind, or the retrieved memory part of the mind, if that was indeed a thing, that he could tell were of the person he imagined. He could remember the way people spoke, recognise them as individuals from their voices alone, but this new inner voice was far too real, it shouted above the other voices, but not by being louder, it was- Miles searched for the word, and the only thing he could think of was, 'three dimensional', all of the other voices were flat, quiet, a memory, he could hear their voice and then visualise the owner delivering their own message from the deepest parts of his memory. Sometimes it was real like a video or tape recording bought to life, replaying a moment that actually happened, sometimes it was dreamlike, new words melding with new images, but the voices were still right. Miles's new voice was wrong and a sure sign he was going nuts.

'You're not going mad!' The voice overwhelmed his thoughts and came as a shock, now it sounded angry, not shouting angry, but powerful angry. Miles imagined Gandalf from the film of The Lord of the Rings standing on the bridge of Khazad Dum and delivering the lines, 'You shall not pass. Another memory and a voice he could recall, he could slot in the pictures, and yet this memory still, wasn't the same as what he was experiencing. Voices from memories are quieter, they don't seem to come from everywhere like this one, they're mind-borne. This one *must* be audible to anyone within earshot.

'I am talking to you and only you! Instead of trying to justify why you're going mad, why don't you talk to me? Maybe you'll get some answers.' The voice was softening now, even though the words seemed antagonistic, they contained within an almost pleading quality. Somehow Miles discerned a sadness there, and Miles felt that he was no stranger to sadness.

'Who are you?' Miles shouted across the deserted shoreline and towards the sea, towards the invisible thing that wanted to have a conversation.

'Actually that's a long story with a rather long answer. I've been called by a few names in the past, but I have never associated myself with any one name. It's for you to decide what you call me. Oh! and I'm not invisible!' The sound came like a soothing, thoughtful reply, that was reminiscent of two old friends talking, conspiring, together in a pub.

'Where the hell are you then?' Miles cut in, screaming the words out and then continued in more subdued exasperation. 'Bugger this, I'm just talking to myself!' He rose to his feet and started walking towards the top of the beach.

'Don't beat yourself up young Skywalker, I'm real, you're real and you *are* talking to me. Please don't go!'

Miles put his fingers in his ears and continued walking.

'I'm sorry, I'm really sorry!'

Miles started to hum an inane tune to himself, feeling the vibration of his tuneless defiance and hearing it through the bones of his skull. Sound, it appeared, didn't have to come in directly through the ears.

'Please!'

The voice was just as there, it overpowered everything he could do to drown it out but it didn't shout to be heard, it just could be heard and now it sounded- desperately lonely and forlorn. Miles had reached the boulders at the top of the beach and for some inexplicable reason he felt a deep sadness inside. He stopped walking and turned to face the shoreline, aware for the first time that inexplicable tears were streaming from his eyes, He'd not felt this sad since- Skip! Slowly he removed his fingers from his ears, and placed his arms down by his sides, no longer humming and no longer able to keep a reign on his emotions, Miles stood there sobbing openly, like a child lost amongst a crowd in a supermarket, parted from his mother and for all he knew, abandoned.

'Please, just come back down onto the beach and sit with me. You're safe and definitely not mad.' the voice lilted.

Miles, eyes streaming and stinging with tears, slowly walked back down onto the beach considering the calm of the words he'd just heard, and totally unsure of where he was meant to be going.

'Just keep coming towards me and I'll tell you when.'

'When what?' Miles faltered the question through his tears.

'When you're with me.' came the disembodied reply. With no directional information from the position of the voice's source, Miles resigned himself to following the instructions he could hear but couldn't place. He walked compliantly, robotically and carefully back towards the wreck, skirting rock-pools and rounding the bigger stones on the shore, so different to his flight up the beach not many minutes before. Miles became aware that he had sustained some damage when he'd fallen, blood and sand had intermingled in the cuts and scratches on his palms and now his hands were a ragged mess. He glanced in distaste at the bright red mess, exaggerated by the presence of moisture, and wondered how sore his hands would be in the morning, all the while following whispered directions in his head.

'Right a bit, watch out for that big rock, keep going, that's the way, you're there,' all in a reassuringly soft voice; the same voice he'd been so scared of, the voice he'd run from, yet now, here he was, following the directions like an automaton, just following the programme like all good robots... or maybe puppets.

'Why don't you sit yourself down again and we can talk, in a while, when you're ready, and if you want to? But you start, when you're ready, I'll not interrupt, I can wait' It wasn't so much a question or an order, more an invitation, one you didn't feel was necessary to refuse or run from. Miles sat, he raised his view away from his numb, bloodied hands and the only thing he saw before him was the hulk of the boat.

Everything seemed quieter now, the drizzle had ceased and there was a stillness to the day. The sound of the murmuring sea remained in the background and the lightest of breezes ruffled Miles's wet hair at the nape of his neck. Occasionally a droplet of water could be heard falling from an unknown source and into a rock-pool, somewhere nearby, but otherwise there was an eerie silence and with that Miles began to believe that his torment was over.

He had time to think over the last few minutes, he looked at his watch and was aware he'd been on the beach for a little over an hour, it would be pitch black in another hour, still plenty of time to just sit calmly and think. He started to disassemble the remembered conversation he'd had in his mind and the weirdest thing that struck him was one word, replaying it over and over, just one word that didn't make any sense, not that any of it made any real sense, but this one word confused him, it wasn't a part of anything really, Skywalker!

'Why did you call me Skywalker?' Miles mouthed it under his breath but it must have been verbally, though Miles wasn't aware, until the voice returned.

'My attempt at a joke, you know? Star Wars, the force is strong with this one!' The voice maintained its evenness with not even a hint of an effected accent trying to do an impression of Darth Vader or whoever it was who delivered the line in the film, Miles couldn't remember, it should have been that sort of raspy, breathy sound that every schoolboy associated with the line and emulated often. It might have been the green guy who spoke in disjointed riddle-words, or was he grey. Darth Vader or Yoda? He couldn't remember.

'Hang on, why would you mention a name from Star Wars? And why didn't I hear it as an impression, like, you know, the little green guy's voice in Star Wars?'

'Maybe because I don't do impressions and anyway, you started it.'

'Started what?' Miles asked.

'The film referencing thing, with your *You shall not pass* thing.' Again there wasn't any discernible change of tone or voice as Miles had heard it from his memory of the film, that commanding, booming, authoritative voice of the actor playing Gandalf the Grey, it was just the voice, calm now that the perceived sadness had melted away. Miles picked at the words in his head and found the 'eureka' moment.

'I didn't say *You shall not pass*, I thought it!' Miles was satisfied that he hadn't quite lost all of his marbles and smiled inwardly, maybe a little outwardly as well.

'You're point being?' prompted the inner voice.

'I'm talking to myself aren't I?' Miles knew the answer he'd imagine before he spoke. He was definitely talking to himself, there was no one there. He was sat in front of an aged, rotting, wooden wreck, on a wet shoreline, talking to- nothing.

'Well, to be brutally honest, from a bystanders perspective, yes, you are, sort of, talking to yourself,' Miles let the voice continue, happy to succumb to the melt-down he was a part of and the lunatic he was turning into, 'You actually don't need to make it so blatantly obvious that you're talking to me, you can do it with your mind instead of using your mouth.' Miles pondered on that. 'Look at us, having a conversation like two old friends in a pub.'

Miles considered the voice's words and didn't miss the reference to the pub, another thing he'd thought about but had never said. Something told him deep inside that he needed to keep talking to himself, to try and garner some information that could be dissected and rationalised, information that might pull him back from the abyss of lunacy he was now heading for. So many images flooded his thoughts but he had to formulate questions and he had to discover what was happening and find the answers. The voice had been called by a few names! Miles had been told that, it didn't make much sense, but here was Miles, talking at a boat's grave.

Calmly Miles thought through a question and pushed it outwards 'What are you then?

'I've considered the answer to that question for years. I'm a dragon at the moment, Miles!' the voice said proudly. Miles sniggered inwardly to himself but the voice didn't react to the open invitation to have a go, maybe he hadn't picked up on it.

'How do you know my name?'

'I don't know, I just do! I knew it as soon as I found you.' the voice replied with a subtle amount of faked concern. Miles was trying to process information as quickly as he were able to. That last reply, in his mind, proved that Miles was speaking to himself and now he was imagining this whole scenario too.

'Hang on, don't get ahead of yourself. Just because I know your name does not mean I'm not real, it doesn't mean I'm all in your head, that I'm imaginary. Yes I am in your head somewhat, a part of you, if you like, but that's the way I communicate. You believe you are talking to yourself at this juncture, so why don't we just sit here and have a conversation and see what develops? At least you're not speaking out loud now, that must be something of a reassurance to you.'

Miles mulled over the offer of a friendly chat with himself or chat with an invisible host, deciding that it couldn't do any more harm, it wasn't as if he'd have to physically speak, it would all go on in his brain somewhere. If he was going mad, no one would know, unless, of course, he started telling other people about it, then he'd surely find himself locked in the back of a white van heading to some secure facility until he could prove his sanity. Miles smiled to himself at that thought, he didn't believe he could prove his sanity regardless of the fact that he was about to have a deep and meaningful with himself or an invisible entity. His thoughts were disturbed by the voice again.

'I'm not invisible, I told you that already!'

'So where are you then?' Miles thought the question expecting a riddle for a reply.

"Right in front of you!' The voice sounded disappointed 'I'm the fetid, rotting, jagged-toothed bones that sit before you. I'm your inanimate wreck that, for a period of incredible violence, was your fossilised, wooden target.'

'I'm sorry.' Miles had no idea why he felt he should apologise to either himself or to an impossible, talking, wreck of a boat. He had certainly perceived a disappointment in the voice he'd imagined and felt he'd used cruel words in his thoughts, but how could he, or anyone for that matter, consider emotions when it concerned a non-living thing. Then again, Miles thought about how his first car made him feel, how he'd named it, how he'd spoken to it, lovingly and with respect, admonishing it only when it let him down. He thought too of his oldest possession, a teddy bear he'd had since he was one year old, Sweep. The conversations he'd had with that stuffed, furry, body, the secrets he had told him, the comfort it had given him and the fact that he'd plied him with male status. The sadness he'd felt when Sweep had been savagely ripped apart by Skip, when Skip was only a few months old and trouble. Sweep had been rebuilt, better than before, by Miles's wife, Julie.

Given eyes to see again, given new life and Miles still spoke to him on occasion. Skip was only a puppy then, beautiful, animate, real, naughty, loyal, and a dog in a million. Tears started to moisten the corners of Miles's eyes as he pictured Skip; Sweep had been returned to him, but Skip never would.

'Im sorry too.' the voice paused for what seemed an eternity before resuming as a knowing whisper. 'I'll leave you for a while, you're too upset, but please come back to me.' There was a beckoning softness to the voice now and the sound trailed away with a finality as the words flowed, it seemed to understand, it showed empathy. Miles believed that it was giving him space, some time to grieve, it was slipping back into the deepest recesses of his mind. Perhaps it was real, probably it was from deep within, but the voice had a conscience and now that there was a tangible silence, there was still hope left. Miles was alone, sat on a wet beach late on a Monday afternoon in January and it was getting far too dark.

Chapter 3

The bus to Kinlochleven from Fort William was, thankfully for Grace Muir, on time and she was glad that she had spent the last half an hour nursing a cup of tea, sat in the warm and dry of a cafe along the high street. Timing it to perfection, she placed the empty cup back onto its saucer, put on her coat, scarf and gloves and, picked up her two, full, food-laden, carrier-bags. She headed out onto the dark, wet, deserted street, making for the bus stop. Once a week she made this journey from her home, to pick up those essentials that would see her through another week, and she always got the same bus into Fort William and the same bus back.

Grace had few friends, but lots of acquaintances, and she lived a solitary existence with only one person to rely upon; herself. The bus pulled up beside her and the suspension lowered causing the boarding deck to become, thankfully, less of a step-up, then the door hissed open. She stepped aboard, struggling with the unwieldy shopping and into the well lit interior, passed Ronnie, the driver, and along the aisle to find a seat against a window, as close to the front of the bus as were available.

'Afternoon Grace,' Ronnie called after her with a chiding taunt to his words. The door closed with a pneumatic hiss and the suspension rose effortlessly.

'Chose a bloody horrible day to venture out, didn't you?' Ronnie continued dejectedly and intoning rebuke, he did not expect a reply, he never got one. Ronnie's face in the rear view mirror watched until Grace was comfortably sat with her bags stowed at her feet, Grace gave the tiniest of smiles towards him in thanks and then, the bus smoothly raised, it accelerated smoothly, moving away from the stop.

The Windows on the bus were dripping wet and steamed up and there'd be no view of the loch or the loch-side houses on the journey home; just the occasional glimpse of a blurred light out in the dark somewhere, or an equally blurry flash of white light from the headlights of a car coming in the opposite direction. As the bus continued on its journey, Grace withdrew into the memories of her own journey.

She was now fast approaching ninety years of age, every year that came and went, much faster than the ones that preceded. Time was like the blur of the headlights she occasionally glimpsed. Five foot two now; the girl she felt was still three inches taller; her short blonde hair and blemish free face with wide, mesmerizingly, blue eyes tended to avoid looking into mirrors nowadays; the person that looked back had grey, grainy, blotchy skin topped by almost white, thinning hair and sunken grey eyes hidden deep within the ever darkening rings of creases. In her preferred memory she was still the beautiful creature she once was. As long as she avoided mirrors. Somewhere along the line Grace had become old, perhaps an image of her own mother in her last years, a mother she'd disappointed, hurt, and Grace had spent a lifetime atoning for her- youth, youth was the only word that sprang to mind. Her memories took her back to when she was fourteen.

Grace ran everywhere, she thought that life was too short to waste it on walking, and, being the last day of school term, it was even more important to run, to get home without squandering any of that precious time, and to plan *her* summer with *her* friends. Boys had just become visible to her and one in particular had caught her eye, by the end of the holidays, he'd be hers, by hook or by crook, as her mother used to say.

As she raced towards the front door of the cottage, her home, her satchel strung over her shoulder, banging awkwardly against her back as she ran, Grace was struck by the strange feeling that something was not as it should be.

On a beautiful, sunny, summers day the cottage appeared dustier and darker somehow. The curtains framed by the windows were still drawn closed and, unusually, the windows were not flung wide open as befitted the day. The door too, left open on any other day like this, was closed. Was anyone home? Grace operated the latch and pushed through the door, she entered the small hallway, and placed her satchel on one of the hooks along the wall, and listened. Around her motes of dust speckled, sparkled and settled, raised by the very act of letting the outside in to the still hallway. From the little kitchen behind another closed door she could hear her mother, sobbing. Something had happened, she was sure.

Grace raced forward and opened the door to the kitchen to face her mother. She was sitting at the small table in the middle of the room looking, to all ends, like the world had crashed in on her, crying piteously into a handkerchief, with a piece of crumpled up, printed paper beneath her free hand. Grace knew it was a telegram, and she knew that there was only one sort of telegram that families received these days. Behind her mother and by the sink, skulking in the shadows, stood before even more closed curtains, the imposingly tall and gaunt minister stooped, holding a teapot and pouring its cold contents away down the sink.

'Reverend.' Grace said courteously with a slight bob of her head. 'Mother?' She questioned without actually saying what she wanted to ask, 'Why is that man here?' Grace knew why the minister was there. The minister turned to face Grace and, after placing the teapot down on the drainer, moved towards her. To Grace it appeared he floated towards her, smoothly and stealthily. His arms flowed away from his sides as he advanced in an open invitation for her to be accepted into his embrace. Grace stepped forwards, her hardened eyes never leaving her mother's broken form, Grace's eyes pleaded for an intervention that never came and she received a pastoral, duteous hug from the minister, as if everything was good in the world, but Grace knew better. After what seemed an eternity, trapped and clamped against the minister, he spoke, always a man of few words, unless it was a part of one of his epic sermons, his baritone voice was now only audible as a whisper heard through his black, musty-smelling, jacket.

'Grace. I'm afraid you're father has been taken from us.'

Her father was in France, fighting for king and country. 'Us!' 'What did *he* mean, 'Us'? She pushed herself away from the minister, backed up, and stood unsteadily in the doorway to the kitchen. The minister had re-assumed his, christ the redeemer, open-armed stance and stood like a huge, beatific, granite statue that barred her way past, preventing any access to the fallen creature that was her mother. Grace turned and fled the house; life was always better running!

'Grace? Grace?' her mothers shattered voice broke free of the sobs, and faded as she ran.

The bus rolled onwards as every microsecond of the encounter of that day burned in her mind. They crossed the bridge at Ballachulish and Grace could tell without even seeing the view; the ambient sound of the bus had changed and there was a pulsation buried deep within the hypnotic rhythm. Reflection of sound from each steel girder, shimmered, as they made their way across the bridge. It always reminded her of where she was. Her childhood home was only a mile or so away now, to her, memories of that day still seemed such a very short time ago. A day when her universe was turned upside down.

Today, Grace ran down to the shore of the loch, usually it was up into the woods to hide, to be invisible when she was upset, today she didn't care who saw her. For a while she ran aimlessly amongst the boulders and small rock-pools that littered the beach, in tears that streamed her cheeks.

It was a warm afternoon with not a hint of a breeze, and, not wanting to go home, she chose to sit down upon a sun-heated rock trying to make sense of everything, she pictured her father but she couldn't picture a life without him, nothing made sense anymore. Her father would never be returning to her, but he must or things would never be the same again, there was no way to make any of this right. Emotions continued to pour from her as she wept a mournful, frustrated lament. When there were no tears left she curled up into a foetal position, clasped her hands together and prayed for Death to take her.

Death didn't take her, but he spoke to her, that afternoon upon the beach. He calmed her, he listened as she ranted on like a spoilt brat. She raged about how it was all so unfair, what were they supposed to do now, where would the money come from, what would her mother do now, how would they live, what about school, why my father. Why? What? How? Why? Death took it all in and soothed her fevered pitch with kind words and a logic she couldn't fault. Finally he said.

'Go home, child. Your mother needs you now, more than you will ever know.'

Grace swallowed some of her childish egotism and went home to be with her mother.

Using the sleeve of her coat, Grace wiped at the window beside her and gazed out through the clearer area of glass. Outside the rain had stopped and the wet streets and pavements reflected the street lamps and lights from houses like gold and silvery mirages bouncing and moving to their own dance. Ronnie was negotiating the bus through the narrow streets of Ballachulish, a place that had changed so much over so few years. Houses that had sprung up in abundance outnumbered, by far, the older properties, some of those still existed, maybe even her mother's old house, but she hardly recognised the area now. And never, would she go in search of her childhood here.

The church was to blame, absolutely the bloody church, and god. At least Death had given her wise counsel in her time of need. What of the Reverend? What had he given her?

Sunday came and wearing her best shoes and darkest dress, face and hands thoroughly scrubbed and her hair clean and combed, wearing a black ribbon to finish off the look, Grace aided and steered her mother to the morning service at the church. Just like on every Sunday, it was a devotion that her mother insisted upon. Grace didn't mind going every week, she rather enjoyed the singing, but after the first hymn-.

The Reverend stood before the congregation glorying in the silence that befell and the attention of his flock, no one dared cough for fear his wrath. This self-proclaimed, pious, great-man proceeded to spout bile and preened; he relished in the nods of agreement and encouragement from the present elders, those sat upon the pews reserved for god's favoured few; he fawned and spewed vitriol. Eschewing the war but sanctifying the heroic death of her father, with right on his side, a death with honour; to be able to be received by god into the kingdom of heaven, and the greatest sacrifice a humble servant of the lord could make. He looked towards Grace's mother with piteous, crawling eyes and lowered his voice to its most dramatic timbre, and said.

'The lord be with you my child!' He was building up to his dramatic finale and Grace couldn't withhold an urgent need to ruin it.

'Judas!' she screamed at the top of her voice. Why that one word? She never knew. Every ounce of energy thrust into just one word, and from a small elfin girl wearing her best dress. And it reverberated dramatically and sounded tumultuous, the sound of a hundred little girls in unison, as the last echoes diminished, Grace ran from the church screaming. The choir of screams following her from the church as she ran.

For the price of thirty pieces of silver. Grace thought, and the journey home continued.

During the school holiday, Grace found she had little time for her friends and, although her mother insisted she go with her to the church, Grace always came up with an excuse or a reason not to, sometimes reacting with a tantrum but always, stubbornly, refusing her mother's wishes. Her mother had taken up the position of house-keeper for a wealthy family in Onich, across the water, and she travelled by bicycle every day to the ferry crossing and payed work. Grace was left pretty much alone, preparing food for the table, or cleaning and maintaining the nest. When she found that there was spare time, she would often find herself upon the shore and in deep conversation with Death, and by invite, Death had started to invade her dreams too.

At the end of the holiday Grace returned to school and her friends there, and one day, in a moment of incredulous stupidity, Grace, in confidence, or so she thought, told her best friend about Death, her mentor. The revelation didn't remain a secret for long, it ravaged through the small village school, caught the attention of the teachers and escaped into the village, finally, reaching the ears of the church.

As with all small communities, everyone knew everyone else's business, and rumours of witchcraft and devil-worship abound. Attempts by the church and its elders to intervene and quiet the situation followed, calling for Grace to seek redemption in the bosom of christ. Grace reacted in the only way she knew how, loudly, violently and vehemently insisting that Death was real and she sought his opinion over that of god's laughable, *chosen,* shepherds. The presbytery became involved and life in the village for Grace and her mother rapidly became untenable.

Her mother's employer, a gentleman of some worth with no stoic religious beliefs, helped save the day. If save could be described as getting them both away from the area, by giving references that helped procure work for her mother in Glasgow, and a continuing education for Grace. The family of two did a moonlit flit with a final settlement payment in their pocket, forfeiting on the rent and never again returning to the glen together.

Seventy-four-odd years ago and it seemed like last week. Her mother had died having never returned; never seen the bridge that crossed the loch now; didn't witness the closure of the ferry nor the slate mine and had never seen the sudden changes the area took when tourism took its firm hold on the place. Grace, however, did return. Her identity hidden by time, and by outliving everyone who knew about her past, and now she lived so tantalizingly close to where it happened, all those years ago.

The bus pulled into the terminus and Grace's destination. With the briefest nod of a thank-you in the direction of Ronnie, she stepped out into the cold, damp, evening air and walked slowly and wearily home. Once through the front door she stowed the shopping in *her* small kitchen in *her* small house, made, and ate, a meagre supper whilst listening to the radio and turned into bed at nine o'clock.

Her dream stripped away the years and she found herself revisiting the conversations, in detail, that she'd had with Death all those years ago. She slept through them and relived them like the film you want to watch again and again, in panoramic vision with surround sound, peaceful and blissful, and a dream she didn't want to awaken from, but awake she did from the euphoria. Looking across at the alarm clock she made an unconscious mental note of the time, it was four o'clock in the morning and she could hear her name being softly called. This hadn't happened since before she left her home in Ballachulish with her mother. To check she was awake, Grace went downstairs, gripping the banister for support, and into the kitchen where she put the kettle on, and made a cup of tea. She splashed icy-cold water, from the tap, onto her face, trying anything that would remove the calling voice or the nightmare going on about her. Just, every now and again, she could hear the voice, calling her name. In the sitting-room she could still hear it, she drank her tea, and tried to ignore the call of Death, but Death kept calling. For once a minute she heard her name called.

Not able to take it anymore, she screamed for it to leave her alone.

The voice stopped as suddenly as it had started, but Grace didn't go back to bed, she remained in the sitting room until the wintry, morning sun, crept through the crack between the curtains. Every thought she had, concentrated upon the time when she was fourteen.

Chapter 4

His arrival back at the motorhome, that evening, proved nowhere near as awkward as he thought it would be. He'd been expecting the silent treatment, maybe even a shouting match, and he wouldn't have blamed Julie if she'd insisted on either.

Miles now felt, somewhat, ashamed at the way he'd behaved earlier that day. Sheepishly, he followed the road into the site and towards his home. The courtesy light, twinkling invitingly above the door, had been switched on for his return, thankfully illuminating his final, sullen, apprehensive approach.

It had taken him nearly an hour to get back from the beach, and he'd spent that hour talking himself through what he'd say to Julie, in defence of his storming off. He wished he could turn back the clock, just a short eight hours, to a time where, maybe, he could have held his temper better in check. Julie would have been struggling with the day's events too, and Miles not once, had comforted her with a re-assuring word or through a supportive action. He felt he'd been selfish, unworthy of her. As Julie's protector he had failed her miserably. Shivering now in the evening chill, he reached out to grip the door handle and accept whatever punishment he deserved.

She'd heard his cautious approach, she could hear the crunch of his boot soles, so loud in the still cold air, through the thin walls of the motorhome. She'd put down the book she'd been reading, face down but still open, and was in the process of removing her reading glasses, when he entered. She was ready! Quite possibly ready to vent her own venom, in his direction, fully expected, fully deserved, but she faltered, stopped herself short and allowed him into the warm, well-lit, interior. Her eyes didn't take long to fixate on his bloodied hands.

'What the hell have you done? I don't believe this, only you-' There was disappointment in her voice but beneath that, there was also an underlying concern.

'I tripped over a tree root or something,' Miles lied, like a schoolboy telling a master that there really hadn't been a fight in the playground, he'd accidentally run onto someone else's closed fist. 'I hadn't got a torch and it's bloody dark out there!' he whined, aware that a little bit of truth might fortify the falsehood.

'Come here, let me see!' The motherliness, caring side came out in her voice and certainly outweighed the disappointment now. Miles obligingly held out both hands, keeping them close to his chest, and he remembered being caned for the first time and not the last, at school. His house-master felt the need to meter out corporal punishment for some fault of Miles that eluded him, and, when asked to hold out his hands, palms up, he was holding them there, close to his heart, just like now, until the master pulled them out from his body to deliver the blows. Julie did just the same now, although to get a better look in a better light, it should have stung as much as the first lash of the cane when she straightened his fingers. He grimaced expectantly and waited for the pain to kick in. It didn't.

'Stop being such a baby,' She was finally able to say. 'I need to check them,' she continued with maternal concern. 'There's too much grit in the wounds, they'll go bad if we don't do something.' Miles just stood there, zipped-lipped, like a child again and he could almost hear the 'tut-tut' that always came from *his* mother when she had been faced with this sort of thing.

'Miles, go and grab a shower, clean yourself up a bit and change out of those clothes, we'll sort it when you get back.'

There was a shower, sink and toilet in the rear of the motorhome, but it was seldom used when the site they were staying on had decent facilities, like this one had. It saved a lot of trouble too. The shower on board was tight and cramped, not much wider than Miles's shoulders, washing, let alone drying, was an art-form here and it invariably resulted in a soaking wet carpet when the curve-around-the-body shower door got caught and opened accidentally during the process. Julie helped gather his wash-bag, already waiting by the sink, a towel airing over the back of the driving seat and a change of clothes, stuffed them into two carrier bags and Miles headed out on the short walk to the amenity block.

When he returned to the van, the atmosphere within it had changed somewhat, Miles felt that the memories of the day had been put on the back-burner, even if it were only for a while. Julie inspected his palms and applied an antiseptic liquid; if his hands should have stung before, they certainly should have stung like buggery now. The sharp pain was thankfully, just not there. Miles gave her his puppy-dog-eyes look, the one that said, I love you.

'Any chance of some medicine that might take the edge off?' Miles asked, with a cheeky, wry smile.

'Only if I join you, and you get them.' she replied.

'But I don't think I can, I'm injured, remember,' He held up his hands, palms up, as to prove the point. 'And anyway, you're nearest.' Miles gazed into her face for any sign there that he was winning, when he saw none, he stood up and fetched down two, cut-crystal, heavy tumblers and a bottle from an overhead cupboard. He placed the glasses on the small occasional table at the side of Julie, removed the cork stopper from the bottle, feigning agony at the effort, and poured out a neat, rather large, whisky apiece.

After dinner, they both picked up their books and read, drinking from their re-replenished glasses. Miles looked up from his book for a moment and watched Julie, he thought back to earlier that evening, he'd without doubt been totally immersed in himself and he had to put matters right. Placing the book down, he crossed to Julie and put his hand on hers. 'I'm sorry.' he said, and at the moment he said it, he understood just how much Julie meant to him.

Julie swung her legs off the divan she was reclining on, making room for him to join her, put her book aside, and Miles sat next to her. He placed an arm around her shoulders and drew her closer, resting her head on his shoulder. 'I really am sorry.' he said again. 'I know you've been putting a brave face on this- I just-.' Miles broke off as Julie turned and kissed him.

'He was your dog, Miles, I understand.'

'He belonged to both of us, and I went off in a hissy-fit without any thought.'

'As long as you don't start making a habit of it, I can forgive you this once.' She kissed him again.

Miles retrieved Julie's glass from the table and passed it to her, after picking up his own and taking a sip he spoke calmly and with warmth, still holding onto the girl he loved. 'Remember when we went back-packing on the Suffolk coastal path, and Skip ran ahead and straight over that cattle grid.' On his shoulder he felt a small nod.

'He nearly made it across, he went straight through the bars with one leg, but his body kept going. We were in the middle of bloody no-where and I thought, christ he's broken his bloody leg, what do we do?' said Julie.

'It's the way he just lay there on the far side of the cattle grid,' Miles added. 'whimpering and lying on his back with his leg in the air.' Miles smiled at the memory.

'And you ran across to him, I thought you'd go through the grid too, when you ran across it.

'I had to get to him, all I could think was, I'd be carrying Skip all the way to a vets, and it would be miles away, and, lets face it, Skip wasn't a lightweight was he?'

'When you got to him, you just felt up and down his legs, over his hips, over his paws and you didn't find anything obvious, Skip just lay there accepting, so you rubbed his belly, and just said come on Skip, up we get. Bloody dog was as happy as Larry after that, straight up and running around at your feet again. Daft thing.'

'I know, well the thing is,' Miles paused. 'You do that for me too, you pick me up when I've done something stupid.' Miles kissed Julie's forehead. 'I love you.'

'You know, Miles, you're a soppy bugger sometimes.' She playfully hit him in the ribs.

They stayed together, Julie nestled into Miles's neck, for a long while, drinking and reminiscing, and whiled away the time before bed.

Sleep didn't come easy that night for Miles, he was exhausted but he couldn't shake off the day nor switch his brain off, allowing it to wander pastures more mundane and more dreamlike. Over and over he replayed all, he perceived, that had happened, he paused it, rewound it, fast-forwarded and tried to edit it into a format, that, like a film with a start, middle and an end, gelled. Eventually he slept, fitfully.

Four o'clock in the morning, what a time to be awoken! Miles thought as he strained to see the digital clock read-out above the domestic switch-panel in the van. He'd been roused by the sound of a name being called, in the distance, probably from the owner of a dog or a cat. An errant animal that hadn't come in from doing their necessaries, he surmised. Settling his head back down to meld into the warm, luxuriant pillow. There it was again! This time he knew, it wasn't coming from outside, it was coming from inside, from inside-him. Startled to attention now, he made vain attempts to try and ignore it. He tried closing his eyes more forcefully in hope that he'd drop off quickly and he might rediscover a state of sleep, but as each, sleepless, minute passed, he heard the calling, softly, but vividly there.

He grew more fearful every time he heard the call, outside it was dark, but inside, inside it was becoming darker still.

'Grace?' a pause then 'Grace?' again, a minute later the call recommenced.

Miles knew who it was causing it but did not want to believe it, having only just pushed all thoughts of his decline into lunacy, to the back of his mind. Here it was again, rearing its ugly head, invading, insistent, incessantly calling, but not him, calling for, who? Grace? He wished it would just go away and he strived to make it 'go away' by thinking those very words, trembling with fear. Whether he had actually succeeded remained unanswered when after an hour, from somewhere, he heard 'Leave me alone!', and the voice he heard, just stopped, as if it had never been.

Miles listened intently, awaiting its return with the covers on the bed pulled up tightly around his neck, held there in an unshakeable grip. He dare not move, nor wake Julie, asleep at his side. He just listened, sweat beading over his whole tightly wrapped torso, eyes large, unable to focus on anything within the dark confines of the van. Other than the iridescent, green digits on the clock. And he waited a long time for the sane release of morning to arrive.

Julie awoke first, according to her that morning, as Miles pretended to still be asleep. When she nudged him gently awake, he made a mini drama of struggling to open his eyes, to be followed by the yawning, full vocal, stretch; not forgetting the smacking, opening and closing of his mouth as he dislodged the distasteful remnants of sleep. Then onto, arching of his back to awaken his body from the *marvelous* night's rest he'd had.

They both washed and dressed, while the kettle on the stove boiled ready for the first coffee of the day. The blinds were opened and the low sunlight streamed into the interior through one of the side windows. Once the coffee was made, Miles took up the kettle and using any steaming water left, poured it into a plastic bowl and proceeded to shave the stubble from his face. On finishing up and toweling dry, he rinsed out the bowl, placed the towel to dry on the back of the only seat without a towel already upon it, and sat, to relish in the bitter bite of his cooling coffee.

The plan for the day, was to follow the road towards the bridge and lunch at the Ballachulish hotel just beyond. A day taking in the views of the loch along the way, the remains of the slate mine, the church, the war memorial, the James Stewart memorial stone and finally the hotel. Miles had seen them all before, but he'd never taken Julie to the hotel and he so dearly wanted to show her the old sign that displayed the costs to use the, now, long-gone ferry. Thirty years ago, on a previous visit, it hung on the public bar wall, or so he remembered. Faded and ageing, it had held his attention for a while, and he had marvelled at the prices, in old money, for taking a tup across, or a cow, or a bicycle. He'd just wished he'd been around then, to have seen it.

Hand in hand, they walked, following the road, in unity once again. The sun shone, giving out some much needed heat to the day and the path shimmered ahead of them with steam, as it slowly dried in the warmth.

At the bridge they climbed the steps to stand in front of the James Stewart monument and read its inscription.

Erected 1911
To the memory of
James Stewart
of Acharn
or
"James of the Glens"
Executed on this spot
Nov 8th 1752
For a crime of which
he was not guilty

Miles didn't know what James had been executed for. The only thing he was aware of, was that it had concerned a man named Campbell, and that the name of Campbell was, so he thought, not well liked in this area. There was a sign in the Clachaig that said, 'No Hawkers or Campbells', but surely that was in reference to the massacre of the MacDonalds, some sixty-or-so, years before. They stood before the monument, reverently, for a few moments, before heading down to the hotel.

The Hotel wasn't quite the same as Miles remembered it, somewhere along the line it had become- more modern, nice still. Manorly and grand on the outside. Turreted and stone built, but inside, the old baronial feel to the place had been softened by new woods and furnishings. Miles made an excuse and went in search of the old public bar he remembered but returned having not found it. The hotel, it seemed, had been bought, and was still being bought, screaming into the twenty-first century, no longer catering for the rough sort that Miles had been a staunch member of, once upon a time. He asked at the bar in the well lit, comfortable lounge they were sat in, about the sign he sought, but the answer he got was, 'It might be somewhere around, I don't know where though.' Miles gave up and retook his, 'sink into a world of luxury', leather-like seat with Julie. They ate, drank and left. Miles, a little disappointed; Julie, really happy with the way the day was panning out.

'Is it okay if I head off for a little walk?' Miles asked Julie who was sat opposite him and reading, back at the motorhome later that afternoon. Miles felt compelled to go and face his demons, he couldn't put a finger on why, but he knew he had to go. Julie pulled at her glasses so they slid down her nose slightly and she could focus better on him.

'If you want. Do you want company?'

'No, I'll be fine, you just carry on with your book. I won't be too long. Thought we might eat out tonight.' he said, as casually and offhand as he could. She smiled in return but inwardly worried, pushed the glasses back up her nose and found her place in the novel once again.

Miles knew where he was going, where he had to go, and, dressed for the cooling temperature as the sun moved towards the horizon, he headed out at a brisk pace towards yesterday's bit of beach. He'd only have a short time before dusk and he didn't want to waste a minute of time in getting there.

The fore-shore was much the same as yesterday, resplendent in its desolation, but today it was surrounded by colour. The mountains, that framed the scene before him, wore only the smallest of fluffy, white clouds on their snow-capped summits like fascinators. The flanks of each mountain were cloaked in hues of purples and reds, hemmed by various shades of green, through a whole spectrum of verdancy at the tree line; trees that almost dipped into the cold waters of the loch. Reflected in the still water, the image reversed, paled and slightly muted, but each mountain had impressed itself upon the water.

Miles made his way across the shore to find his seat amongst the detritus. He didn't know where to start, how to begin a conversation with a skeletal boat. In his mind, a part of him knew how impossible this all was, but that part of his conscience wasn't strong enough to rule anything out; curiosity had won the day. A part of him hoped, still, that absolutely nothing would happen, but, strangely, he felt able to accept it, if, indeed, something weird did happen and, he'd keep it well hidden from Julie. Miles thought back to the early hours of that morning and spoke loud the name he'd heard, questioningly but quietly.

'Grace? *Grace?*'

'I'm glad you're back Miles, I didn't know whether you would be.' The voice was sitting gently in his mind, there was no aggressive taking over of it, it was just there, nestling in, as if it had always been there. 'Are you all right? Your hands? Yourself?'

Miles mulled the question over before replying. 'Yes I'm fine, but it was you who woke me up, wasn't it?' Miles already knew the answer but just needed it confirming.

'Yes it was, but I didn't mean to wake you. I wanted to speak to Grace but I seem to be having a few problems there.'

'Who's Grace?'

'Someone I knew a long time ago.'

'But you woke me up, calling her name, I couldn't get back to sleep, you scared the crap out of me.'

'I can only apologise, I won't do it again,' Miles wondered at the truth of that, Miles also wondered about how calm he felt, given that he was talking to himself, and out loud.

'I told you,' came back the voice. 'You don't have to speak out loud for me to hear you.'

'But that's what I feel more comfortable with- you-you're- robbing me.' Miles said, exasperation tingeing his voice. 'Otherwise you have complete control over me, you can steal my thoughts, take the ones I don't want you to know, take the ones I haven't thought through enough, as complete and gospel, and then you'll misconstrue what I meant to say.'

'I won't, because I can access all of your thoughts, you formulate the words almost without thinking and *I* can keep up. Miles, I know what you want to say, or ask, as soon as you think it. What would you really like me to do? How might we resolve this discomfort you feel?' Miles thought for a few seconds, formulating. He knew that the voice was listening, but he had to dis-associate himself with the voice in some way, otherwise, he really might loose what remained of his sanity.

The voice remained patiently quiet, not commenting on Miles's 'impending loss of sanity' and waited for Miles to speak.

'Can you tell if I'm mouthing words, without vocalizing them?'

'I've never tried.' the voice said, deep inside-somewhere. 'Why don't we give it a go?'

'But you have to stay out of my head while we do it or it's cheating me, can you do that?'

'I don't know whether that's possible but, I promise you, I will only react to your mouthed words if I can. Hopefully you'll feel better talking to me then. Lets give it a bash.'

Miles struggled to find a way to test the voice, struggled even to know what to say, so he thought about dragons, pictured them breathing fire, wreaking havoc, flying low over fields full of crops, setting them alight, killing the villagers, to be finally bested by a knight on a white charger, with a lance. Then he mouthed his question silently.

'What's it like being a dragon?'

Chapter 5

'What's it like being a man?' the voice replied rhetorically. 'You ask a very difficult question, Miles. I've sort of always been a dragon, I know nothing else. I just, am, a dragon, in the same way that you are a man. The best answer I can give is, it's okay being a dragon, I'm hap-'

Miles cut him off and mouthed. 'So why do you think you're a dragon then? You did say that, you had considered what you might be, and then decided upon, that you were a dragon.'

'This is a new one on me, Miles. I'm trying, desperately, to stay out of your mind, trying hard to only perceive your thoughts when you, consciously, command your lips to move, and no-one, no-one, has ever butted in to my train of thoughts like you just have. This is quite the novelty!' the voice said with bemusement and continued.

'The reasons I know I am a dragon are because, on the first hand, there aren't many of us left. There used to be hundreds of us and we would talk to each other, even though we were separated by huge distances, we'd talk with our minds. These days, I call out to my kind and I can hardly sense their existence. Very rarely do I have a conversation with my own nowadays, I think there are only a handful of us left throughout the whole world. Secondly, I am so very old. No other being on this planet lives as long as a dragon and, counting back the summers and winters, I reckon to be over seventeen-hundred years old, probably older than that. Time doesn't have too much meaning for a dragon.' Miles listened to the voice intently and noted a slight sadness, hinted at, during those final words.

'How long do dragons live?' Miles asked, and regretted it immediately because the question was rudely given and he guessed he already knew the answer.

The voice answered 'I don't know, Miles, but there are so few of us alive now, I fear I am towards the end of my days.'

'What about young dragons?'

'There are no young dragons, Miles. All dragons are the same age, born on the same day at the same time, we are the first and the last, and when the last dragon dies, we're gone. There will be no more dragons.' The voice indicated with little feeling, the demise of his kind, just acceptance. 'Miles, I have a notion that you don't believe I'm a dragon. Why?' he questioned.

Miles re-visited, in his mind, the images he'd pictured a few moments before, and responded. 'I thought dragons could breathe fire and fly.'

'I certainly can't do that.' the voice replied with amazement.

'Dragons come from eggs, they grow big and scaly, they have wings and have a penchant for gold.' Miles stated as he bought back everything he thought he knew about dragons.

'How have you come upon this- knowledge of what a dragon is?'

Miles wondered himself, 'Films and books, stories.'

'That's just it, Miles. Have you ever seen a dragon in real life before?'

'Well, no.'

'Do you know of anybody that has seen a dragon in real life?

'No.'

'So now you've met your first dragon, do you see me as the flying about type, or laying eggs?' he guffawed.

'Not really, I see you as-' Miles picked out every detail he could discern about the skeletal remains of the wooden boat in front of him. 'I see you as-' how could he say it again, but he saw no way of softening what he was faced with, so delivered his assessment. 'You're the skeletal remains of a boat, you're paint has virtually all gone, you consist of slowly rotting timbers, half buried and, you are covered in seaweed, barnacles and mussels. Oh, and I'm talking to you!'

'You're still having problems with whether I exist compared against, whether you're talking to yourself then, I see.'

'Too bloody right I am!' Miles shot back.

'Does it really matter? Would it make you feel better if you knew you were talking to yourself? Or would you rather feel that you were talking to a dragon, me?' Miles couldn't decide which he'd prefer, either way, he was probably three grapes short of the full bunch. He decided it didn't matter either way.

'Can we skirt around the decision making bit, at least until I get my head round all of this?' Miles asked. 'Can't we just continue like, it's not important.'

'Of course we can, if that's what you want. It's not like you're running away anymore, is it?' the voice said understandingly. 'My outer visage, is as you've described, Miles, but I am a conscious entity, a living being. Not breathing and wandering about as you are. I reside within the confines of these, skeletal remains, as you put them, but no less alive than you are, with choices to make and thoughts of my very own.'

'Can you leave the confines of your- visage?' Miles asked with intrigue.

'When I'm ready, I'll leave and take up a new habitat, it's my choice when, it's my choice where.'

Miles looked towards the bridge and the horizon where the sun was rapidly disappearing below it. He knew he couldn't let Julie down again. Just an orange glow to show where the sun had shone its final rays, remained and the sky, around it radiated red and reflected in the loch. 'Look.' He pointed. 'Can you see the sunset?

'With my whole being, Miles.' the voice sounded gladdened, as if his entire existence had been waiting for this moment.

'Do you have eyes to see through?'

'Not as you have, Miles. As I said, I see the sunset with my whole being.'

'Like a god?'

'No! Like a dragon!'

'I have to go, I've made a promise that I can't break. You've given me a lot to think over.' And as an afterthought. 'Please don't wake me up tonight. Please!'

'Will you be back?'

'Yes.'

'Good. Then we can talk about whatever you wish, and maybe, some good will come of it. I really don't mean to harm you Miles, I'm here to look after you. I've made that mistake before, not on purpose you understand. I need to put right an error of judgement I made, and I know I can't do it alone, Miles.'

'Is it something to do with Grace?'

'Yes it is, Miles. But there's time for that conversation yet.' The dragons voice tailed away, and seemed to be deep in reminiscence. Miles got up and started heading up the beach whilst it was still light enough to find his way safely. 'Goodnight, Miles.'

'Goodnight, Dragon.' It came so easily to say those few words out loud.

Heading back to Julie, roll-up cigarette clamped between his lips, Miles felt strangely elated. He'd controlled the conversation he'd just had with the dragon, and, he was warming to the idea of future contact with the dragon; even if he was talking to himself. He was looking forward to the next encounter.

With a spring in his step, he returned home. Julie watched him as he entered.

'You look like the cat that got the cream.' Julie said, and Miles smiled even more.

'Are you nearly ready to go?' he asked.

'Almost.'

It didn't take Julie too long to get ready and after a few minutes, dressed for the cold evening promised by the blue-sky day that they'd just had, they were heading along to Glencoe, to the Gathering, a restaurant and pub to the side of the Glencoe Inn. The ice that had formed on the pavement, crunched and crackled beneath their feet like sparkling fireworks, and the air was bitingly cold as they walked, arm in arm.

Inside the large restaurant, they sat at a table quite close to the bar, by the log burner in the corner. Miles bought the drinks and returned with them and they chatted and planned for the next day. From the menu, they selected what they wanted to eat and Miles stood up, again, to order it, returning with additional drinks.

The food arrived and they ate heartily. The portions here definitely weren't on the small side, but even though Miles was enjoying his food, he couldn't help but look across at another couple's table and what they were eating. Lobster! He wished he'd chosen that.

'You never change, Miles.' said Julie, smiling at him. 'The grass is always greener somewhere else, isn't it?'

'Julie, what do you think a dragon looks like?

'That's a bit out of left field.' she replied, bemused. 'In fact, that's out of the park, Miles.'

'No, humour me, what do you think a dragon looks like?' Julie looked thoughtful for a moment.

'Well, other than, they aren't real, I suppose they would have wings and, I dunno, be really big with long tails and- scaly skin.'

'That's what I thought.' Miles said, but the intonation of his voice spoke that he knew better now.

'You sound like you've seen a dragon.' she smirked.

'No, no.' he replied with a generalism and hoped unconcern. 'It was just something I was thinking about, on my walk, you know. We all *know* that dragons are mythical.' He tried to make it sound so, matter-of-factly. 'The biggest thing that ever flew was probably, a pterodactyl or something like that, and they've been extinct for millions of years. So where did we, the human race, get the idea of a dragon from?'

'Okay, you want to talk about dragons. You're weird, Miles.'

'Not just dragons, I just want to know your thoughts. On other stuff as well.'

'Like what?

'Like-' Miles didn't know if he was pushing this too hard but continued unabashed. 'Could there be a form of life that- doesn't reproduce, that appears on earth, and, once its lifecycle is over, becomes no-more. It just ceases to be?'

'Bloody hell, Miles. What have you been smoking?' The smile on her face had broadened into a grin.

'It's just something I was thinking about and I wanted your opinion on.'

'Well, at least your keeping it grounded.' She giggled and took a sip of her drink. 'At least it's on earth not some other planet, the one you're from!' Julie couldn't contain her laughter any more, she nearly choked and she spat her drink back into the glass. Miles passed her a napkin to wipe away the gin that was dribbling down her face, and his face took on a look like there had been a girl he fancied and she had just shunned his advances, in front of his peers too!

'What's this about, Miles?' she asked, attempting to straighten herself up. Miles tried a different tack.

'It's in the book I've been reading.' he fibbed. 'There might be creatures on earth that have been mistaken for- no, thats not the word, re-invented, thats better, re-invented as dragons, or unicorns or, phoenixes. Just because, what they really are is impossible to quantify as real in our minds.' Miles finished and was quite happy with the form of what he'd said.

'I thought the book you were reading was about the Outer Hebrides.' she said.

'Well, it is, but there was a slight reference and it got me to thinking.'

'You've come up with that, from reading a fictional, cop-based drama located in the Outer Hebrides!' Julie stated. 'You are the only person I know, who'd disappear into a novel of that sort, and come out of it wanting to know more about- life-forms on earth and mythological creatures and, *dragons*.' she over-emphasised the final word loudly.

Miles smiled at her reply and shrugged his shoulders resignedly. At that moment, the waitress turned up, to clear the table. They both helped pile the crockery and she disappeared back towards the kitchen.

'I couldn't help but overhear.' the girl behind the bar said apologetically but keenly, in a broad Scottish accent, behind Miles's back. Miles turned about to face her. 'Mythological creatures and dragons?' Miles saw no reason to ignore her, she might even help to make Julie take it a little more seriously.

'Yes, mainly dragons.' he began, a little unsure now that he'd revealed his major interest. She opened the hatch in the bar-top and, stepping through, approached them. Julie shot Miles a glance that said, with incredulousness, 'Really!'

'There's quite a few places around here called Dragon this or Dragon that. The golf course at Ballachulish is called the Dragon's tooth golf course. I've also heard a story about another, sort of, mythological creature.

My grandmother used to tell it and it involved someone from the area from when she was a child, here.'

'Really! Here!' Miles encouraged. The girl was young, probably in her twenties, and she bore on her arms, tattoo sleeves. It was a most outlandish feature and Miles found it difficult to move his eyes away from them. She was undoubtably very pretty, he noticed when he forced his eyes up her petite frame and took in the rest of her, her blemish-free face, the face of youth, with a small, perfect nose, studded with a small diamond on one side; short dark, brunette hair that kissed her shoulders just, and a paleness to her skin that might, in anyone else, have only existed through the application of make-up, Miles wasn't sure. If it was make-up it was bloody good, but the overall effect was one of innocent beauty; until his attention was drawn back down to her arms again. Miles couldn't understand why she'd ruined her arms, in his opinion. There were so many designs, each, bleeding into the next, and none of them standing alone, until he started to take more notice of them, picking out the odd skull here, or a celtic symbol. And then he saw it. Deeply embedded beneath the tattoos, the skin on her arms and hands wasn't smooth, it was like that of a reptile. Miles hadn't noticed it at first, the tattoos covered- something there that she didn't want to display. He looked at her hands, the backs of them equally as smothered in ink as her arms and, gazing through the ink, realised that she bore horrendous burn scars. Miles's expression must have reacted because she put her hands, quickly, out of view.

'I'm sorry.' Miles said, as the pain that she must have gone through, finally, dawned upon him. Not just the physical pain, but the mental one too, and he wasn't helping much by staring. He hoped his apology had been accepted more like, he'd had a problem with his hearing and didn't quite catch that. But in the way she started towards the safety of the bar again, he knew it wasn't the case.

'Please tell us about what happened, here.' he pleaded softly, raising his arms slightly and straightened his fingers, shrugging as if to encompass the whole of the area they were in.

The desired effect, fortunately, was achieved, and the girl didn't escape behind the relative safety of the bar.

Stopped in her retreating tracks she appraised Miles and Julie for a few seconds. 'Tourists! But? Something new, something different, about these two!'

Chapter 6

At that inconvenient moment, or so Miles reckoned, the couple sitting at the next table to them, the lobster eaters, got up and approached the girl.

'Can we pay for our meal?' the man asked, fiddling to retrieve a card from his, already-open, wallet.

The girl re-assumed her position behind the bar and totted up their bill, she took the card and entered its details, then passed the card-machine across for the transaction to be authorised by the card-holder. All the while she delivered the usual pleasantries. 'Everything alright for you?' and 'I'm glad you enjoyed the meal.' she cooed. The man filed the card and receipt, pocketed his wallet, and the couple finally left.

Then, 'bugger me!' thought Miles. If someone else didn't go up to the bar to order more drinks, and coffees at that! The girl would be occupied for ages. She looked passed the new customer and with a tiny shrug, that spoke volumes, said how she finished her shift at nine and hadn't forgotten them. Miles smiled back at her weakly and turned back to face Julie.

'Fancy bringing her into the conversation!' Julie scolded in a hushed voice. 'She's only a kid. And just look at those tattoos. She's a mess!'

Miles drew closer to Julie and whispered. 'The tattoos are to hide her scars, her hands and arms have been badly burnt.' Julie tried to see passed Miles and see the scars for herself. 'Don't Julie! Don't, just ignore it, please! It's nothing to do with us!' he pled as quietly and forcefully as he could. Julie turned back to face him.

'I didn't realise.' she said apologetically.

Miles and Julie sat chatting about, of all things, the likelihood that the Loch Ness monster may have actually existed, or may not have. Surprisingly, they had very similar views and they agreed that, although they would like it to be real, they both doubted it, given that every piece of photographic evidence was either proven fake, proven a natural phenomenon or, too grainy or distant an image to be taken seriously.

In a few days time their holiday would take them to Fort Augustus at the southern extremity of Loch Ness. A place that they had visited last year during the summer. Miles shuddered at the thought, remembering how crowded it was and hoped that this time around, it would be less populated by the touristy types, types he didn't associate himself with.

At nine o'clock, as promised, the girl behind the bar finished her shift and a young man took over from her, she came and stood between the touristy types that were Miles and Julie.

'Would you like something to drink?' Miles offered.

'Thank you, yes. Half a lager would be nice.' she said. Miles got up from his chair and ordered a round of drinks at the bar. Returning, he placed the drinks onto three beermats on the table, and invited the girl to sit at the table with them, motioning towards a chair. She removed her awful fawn-coloured apron with leather ties placing it over the back of the chair and sat. With the apron gone, her legs were more revealed beneath the tight black miniskirt she wore, Miles found it quite intimidating and struggled to raise his eyes from her satin-smooth legs, quite thankful when they were no longer on display and under the table. 'I'm Mhairi, by the way.' She smiled at Miles.

'Julie.' Miles pointed without any reason and awkwardly. 'Miles.' his pointed finger turned inwards towards himself, equally as pointless. 'I've never heard of that name before, not the way you pronounce it anyway.' before continuing. 'You were about to tell us of something that happened here.' He prompted her to speak.

'Well, you'd know it better as Mary in the way that it's spelt, but its pronounced to rhyme with bar and ree like in tree.' Mhairi watched the two customers getting to grips with her name, both mouthing silently the new words. "You were on about mythological creatures. I don't want to offend you, can I just ask a question first. Are you-' she looked them, in turn, straight into the eyes, Miles then Julie, but stayed looking at Julie as she carried on. 'Are you strictly religious? Because the story involves the devil.'

'Miles hasn't got a religious bone in his body.' Julie said giving an honest opinion and smiling towards Miles. 'I have a sort of faith, but wouldn't put myself down as being a devout follower. I'm certainly not a zealot, Miles reckons I'm a Methodist.'

Faith assured, Mhairi started her story.

'This all happened during the war, it's something my Grandma told me when I was younger, and other people have been told it, by their parents or grandparents, too.'

She took a sip of her drink, Miles settled back in his chair slightly and Julie rested her elbows upon the table, looking on intently. 'There used to be a young girl who lived in Ballachulish, just down the road from here, and she used to talk to the devil. Apparently, on the last day of school term, she got home and was given the news that her father had died in the war. After that, she went slightly mad. I can understand that a bit, but she reckoned that she had talked to the devil, or death as she called it, somewhere out on the beach.' Miles perked up at the mention of the beach and sat forward slightly. 'It was a lot more religious here then, of course, everyone used to go to church on a Sunday; there were very few people who didn't. On one Sunday morning service, the young girl blasphemed to the minister, screamed, and ran from the church. Everyone reckoned she was the spawn of satan after that. However, she never stopped insisting that she spoke to the devil, the whole time she was here, and on more than one occasion too. They couldn't school her, I think the school may have been tied closely to the church then, and the girl wouldn't go anywhere near the church after that. Her mother did, but the girl was always absent.' Mhairi paused.

'What happened to her after that?' Julie asked.

'No-one really knows. The girl and her mother just disappeared. By all accounts, when their house was entered shortly after their disappearance, it was still full of their stuff, clothes, personal belongings, that sort of thing. They'd just vanished, like the crew from the Marie Celeste, you know, hot cup of coffee steaming away and food on the table. The church did quite well out of it though, for quite a long time after, it was rammed with people every Sunday. Everyone thought that it was prudent to attend services; even if they didn't usually go, they made that extra effort. Allegedly, the reverend they had here then was a hard-liner, and no-one dared cross him. There were even rumours that the reverend, or the church, had done something to the girl and her mother to get rid of them, but no-one knows for sure, and no-one wanted to be the one to accuse the minister of anything. Most people just went along with the belief that the devil had taken them for his own.'

'What do you think?' Julie asked.

'I used to think that it was just a story, to make you say your prayers at night. But now I think it's true, what happened, because everyone thats from around here, knows the story, and the story never alters, whoever tells it.' Mhairi said, with her honest appraisal.

'Do you think that the story has altered at all over time? Like with Chinese whispers.' Miles quizzed Mhairi, but it was Julie that answered on her behalf.

'I doubt it, love. There are only three generations that the story has passed through, it's all too recent to be misconstrued.'

'So what interest do you have in mythology?' Mhairi directed the question towards Miles.

Miles took a few seconds to answer, he took a sip of whisky, creating time to think. He knew he had to tell a white lie. 'I've been reading a book and there was a reference to a dragon in it.' It was Mhairi's turn to sit forward a little more though she couldnt remember why it was important.

'Go on, tell Mhairi about your impossible life-form, the one that doesn't breathe or reproduce.' Julie said with a perceptible sneer.

'A what?' Mhairi asked a little confused.

'Well, I was wondering whether a thing like- say a dragon, might not be the picture we have in our minds of what a dragon looks like, but something that defies any explanation. It could be a creature that doesn't adhere to any rule that humans can comprehend. Perhaps it doesn't breathe, maybe its invisible, so it becomes a dragon in name only, and those that haven't seen this creature, put their own stamp on it. Give it wings, have it breathing fire, and it enters into mythology.'

'Well it's bloody invisible, isn't it Miles!' Julie rebuked, laughing. Miles loved the way Julie's face lit up when she laughed, but he really wished she wouldn't sometimes.

Miles looked at the face of Mhairi and saw that she wasn't laughing, she looked, buried and deep in thought.

The three of them sat there in discussion for a while, but after Julie's last comment, Miles had seen fit to change the subject matter somewhat.

Miles and Julie told Mhairi something of themselves and their holidays in Scotland, then they asked Mhairi about what it was like, being and living, in Glencoe. Mhairi told them about attending school at Glencoe primary then, as she got older, having to travel every morning to Kinlochleven High school, away in the next valley. Once her school days were over, she found herself studying art and design at the University of Glasgow before returning to Glencoe. Her main job, though, wasn't here. By day she worked at a craft shop in the village, designing and selling items, some, she had produced herself. She invited them to visit while they were staying.

'Do you have children?' Mhairi asked out of left park.

'No.' Julie answered, 'It wasn't through lack of trying, but we never did.'

'That's a shame, I think that if you'd have raised kids they'd be weirdly interesting. I hope that doesn't offend?'

'Not in the slightest.' Said Miles, wondering how weird could be construed as interesting or good.

'I've spent most of my life being considered weird, comes with the territory of trying to be an artist, I suppose.'

'What do you do, as an artist?' asked Julie.

'Whatever I have to that makes money but I favour acrylics. If you pop by the shop you'll see.'

The topic of conversation moved on and Miles and Julie listened intently as Mhairi spoke. It didn't escape either's attention that Mhairi came across as being exceedingly well educated and erudite. They laughed, they told jokes and they behaved like old friends, too long in parting. The conversation was varied and easy going, no subject seemed taboo and time passed quickly in her company.

Eventually, too soon, the evening came to a close. 'I'll be wearing trousers tomorrow, Miles.' Mhairi said smilingly and they went their separate ways.

'What was that about?' asked Julie.

'Well she has got great legs.' Miles replied and received a cursory slap.

At midnight Mhairi MacInnes was sat alone in her small studio at the rear of her small home holding a pencil in her right hand, in her left hand she clutched a cup of coffee that had long since gone cold.

In front of her, taped to a board on an easel, a large piece of paper remained untouched, not a mark of pencil or pen had blemished its surface. Around her the accoutrements of an artist lay. Half empty acrylic-paint tubes, pots full of brushes, palette knives, pens and pencils. Leaning up along the walls, artworks, some finished and ready for framing, some incomplete and awaiting inspiration. Mhairi, seemingly, sat staring straight through the whiteness of paper before her, devoid of any creativity, like trying to see the image within a magic eye picture

She thought back to earlier that evening, the way she'd backed herself away to hide, after Miles had seen through her inked skin to the scars beneath. She'd not thought about those scars for quite a few weeks now. The quiet season in the glen gave her time to almost forget about them, and she was unlikely to meet very many people, at this time of year, who didn't already know they were there; the people who knew, accepted and ignored them. Today, however, Miles had seen through them, she'd seen that slightest hint of recognition in his eyes.

For some reason, she couldn't explain, she felt drawn to Miles, moreover, she felt an affinity with him, there was something in his eyes, something there that eluded her, and she wanted to know, what? To top it all, she was slightly concerned at Miles's knowing of her scars, but not in the same way of other people who had seen them before him. Miles's recognition hadn't changed anything. She was intrigued by him.

Rolling the clock back, she closed her eyes and remembered the day that ruined her childhood.

Four years old in the back seat of her fathers car and heading to Inverness and her Aunts house for a party. Her older brother, Ross, sitting next to her and taunting. Her fathers face, turning away from the road for rapid moments, to shout at them to be quiet. Her mother turning sideways in her seat to try and slap Ross on his legs and allow her father to watch the winding road. Eventually peace was declared and Mhairi looked out through the window and watched Loch Ness pass by. Outside it was a clear but frosty morning, and the trees swayed heavy with frost.

The party was for the celebration of halloween. Samhain, her father had called it, the time that heralded the transition of summer into winter, light into dark and life into death. The spirits would run free tonight, but it was all the same these days. Instead of turnips turned into lanterns, there'd be tea-candles inside carved pumpkins; instead of the children running about dressed disguised as mini imps or horrors of the night, the children would be dressed in their choice of fancy dress; instead of guising, there would be trick-or-treating. The traditional apple-bobbing would be there, but they called it apple dookin', the same rules, the same game. Mhairi was excited though.

Her aunt had made for Mhairi a most fantastic costume for the festivities, using odds and ends of material that she'd found, stitching them all together and producing a furry-red, padded, full-bodysuit, resplendent with a red-hooped aerial and a television tummy, to boot. Mhairi couldn't wait to try it on, she'd be Po from the Teletubbies, and she even had a little red scooter to finish off the effect. Once zipped inside, Mhairi whizzed about the house on her scooter, singing the theme song to the Teletubbies, probably getting on everybody's nerves. Eh Oh!

Early in the evening, all the children there were escorted around the neighbourhood, trick-or-treating, bringing back to the house the profits of their efforts with sticky fingers and dirty mouths. Tea was set and sausage rolls were devoured, followed by jelly and blancmange. Games were played in the conservatory and the adults joined in. Quite possibly it was more fun to watch your father try and eat a treacle scone, suspended on a string, without the use of his hands. Parents were getting into the spirits, if not the spirits. Outside everything was readied for the finale.

At the bottom of the garden they all gathered and a huge bonfire was lit, sparklers were passed around, and once lighted, the children ran about waving them, writing their names in the air in a cascade of brilliant-white sparks and the starriest glow, giggling, shouting and joyous. They ran around the fire in screaming, careering circles. Then Mhairi stumbled, she saw the ground racing up to meet her, she shut her eyes, put her arms out to catch the floor, she didn't see the fire, she didn't see the flames, she couldn't open her eyes, and she didn't stop screaming.

On the opposite side of the fire, away from Mhairi, her parents hadn't seen the fall or the conflagration. The other children continued their rampaging, the retinas of their eyes blurred, and burned with the images of the brilliant swords of light they brandished. One by one the lights died and extinguished, the screams of glee stopped, and were replaced by screams of horror, to join Mhairi's own screams of agony.

Racing to her, the adults used their hands to try and extinguish the flames, their coats, their bare hands, anything, to extinguish the flames that engulfed the arms and hands of the little, red-suited, Mhairi, Someone fetched a tub of water, last seen containing apples, and finally doused the inferno. Her mother tried to remove the suit that she wore, the red suit with sewn-in mitten-hands, and as the sleeves were pulled down, Mhairi's skin went with them. The screaming continued for days.

Her infant years; those years when you ran and played, with no concerns whatsoever; those formative years, where you learnt and grew, through experience and teaching; came to an abrupt halt. Instead, she travelled backwards and forwards to hospital, underwent countless operations to re-cover the backs of her hands and her arms with skin, and she was always in pain.

As she grew, the skin on her arms didn't, even more grafts were demanded and even more pain resulted. The worst though, were her fingers, she couldn't bend them to make a fist, nor even pick up a pencil to hold it in a grip, her hands were rigidly held straightened, like they were trapped in a vice. Operations to release them continued through her teens followed by innumerable physiotherapy sessions. In turn, more operations and more physio. But with every treatment, there was always more pain!

Mhairi dropped the pencil from her artists' grasp, the thin wooden casing hit the tiled floor and bounced, the lead shattered in numerous places and the tinkling sound, when it landed, broke her reverie. She flexed the fingers on her right hand trying to re-install some control and looked down forlornly at the now useless pencil.

In front of her the white piece of A3 held onto one scrawled word, deeply embedded, 'Shit'. She couldn't remember writing it but it certainly described her memories of her childhood.

Chapter 7

'You miss Skip, don't you?' Julie asked, as they teetered and balanced, their way back from the Gathering on the hard, iced pavement.

'Yes, I do.' Miles replied, suddenly hit again by the feeling of loss. Miles had given little thought to Skip today, and he abruptly felt guilty. What would Skip think? Miles knew, Skip wouldn't think anything. But to ignore the possibility was akin to deleting him from ever having existed.

'Do you think it's the right time to get another dog?' she asked. Miles could not picture there ever being a right time to replace Skip. Even though it had been a few months since that fateful day, and Skip's ashes since, held in the little wooden cask, had waited, discarded but waiting; sat upon the mantle above the fire, ready for the day to come to be scattered; ready to be in the only place they felt he belonged, that wasn't with them. Miles did not think that there would ever be a dog that could replace Skip.

'One day, love.' Miles said grimly. 'It's too soon at the moment.'

Miles thought back to how he hadn't been apart from Skip the whole of Skip's life. Even when Miles had been admitted to hospital, he'd found a way to see Skip, even if it were only for a short time. Julie had bought Skip with her to the hospital for visiting, and left him in the back of the car in the car park. She'd found a wheelchair and kidnapped Miles from the ward, only an hour after Miles had had major surgery, just so Miles could be with his best friend for a few moments. Miles always believed that his rapid recovery, from the operation he'd had, was down to not being apart from Skip.

Back in the safety of the motorhome Julie read the final few pages of her book and Miles poured himself a nightcap from the rapidly evaporating contents of a bottle. 'So it was to be shopping in Fort William, tomorrow.' he thought, gazing longingly, into the remains of the amber liquid held within the cut-crystal.

The glass now empty, its clear flanks matted and smeared by the grease from the fingertips that had cradled it so closely; the book now closed, only the cover trying to re-open itself like a muscle memory. Miles and Julie retired to bed. The end to a rather strange Tuesday.

Grace found it very difficult to concentrate on anything that day, after the events of earlier that morning. She tried to busy herself about the house, but she had no enthusiasm for it. The voice that called her name, that plaintive voice, clawed her memories of her life into the daylight.

She'd never forgotten her association with Death after moving away from the glen, even though the voice couldn't be heard anymore. It was ideal, at the time, because she had far more pressing concerns; rapidly having to learn a new language, a mixture of Scottish and English, just to survive. Her native Gaelic wouldn't help her blend into 1940's Glasgow life.

And eventually, she'd come back home to the glen, or as near as she dared, having been schooled in Glasgow, worked in Glasgow, married, miscarried, and divorced in Glasgow, culminating in her retirement; all in Glasgow. After retirement, she'd returned. After a simple, frugal existence in Scotland's second city, she had accumulated enough to make her retirement, comfortable, not lavish; Grace didn't do lavish! And now, twenty-something years later, years of peace, years without worry, the thing knew she was here. She could not let him in again!

Her whole life, after leaving Ballachulish to now, had been spent re-attaining and preserving a normality. What had happened before, could not happen again. She'd spent too much energy and time, ridding herself of the stigma that stuck like glue. She'd made peace with her mother, and her mother had been proud of her. She'd picked herself up, dusted herself off, and she'd been respected for it.

At Nine-o'clock that evening, after achieving nothing through the day bar feeding her cat, she put all of her thoughts on low heat, and on the back-burner, and she retired to bed. The end to a rather strange Tuesday.

Mhairi put down her mug, crossed her fore-arms and gripped her elbows. Under her fingertips she felt the skin of her arms, they weren't smooth and satin-like; hers were like braille. With her fingers, she traced the lines of the scars that indicated one skin graft or another, so many skin grafts that she had lost count. She located areas where her fingers dipped and delved into smoothed hollows, and areas where there were hardened, raised, gristly lumps. In disgust, she stopped the exploration and ceased the line of thought.

Tomorrow, she'd keep an eye out for Miles and Julie, they were different from the regular tourists she'd met. Yes, Miles had seen the scars, but his reaction wasn't what she'd expected, he hadn't wanted to intrude by asking about them, and he hadn't ignored her completely after seeing them; he'd seen them, he'd not judged. One of the things that drove Mhairi livid, were those people who made it so damned obvious that they'd seen the scars, and either, felt the need to talk about them, like discussing them would make them go away, or, avoiding any continued conversation with her, for fear they'd say something that would upset her; she wanted neither. Miles, seemingly weird and Julie, seemingly normal, verging on weird through association, had given neither, and they'd had a pleasant evening.

'Dragons though?' thought Mhairi. 'What a curious thing to discuss with a total stranger.' Somewhere inside though, a niggling seed of recognition germinated. Dragons! She couldn't quite put her finger on it, something forgotten from her childhood, it was locked away in a dormant part of her mind. She would find it and bring it back into the light. Like everything lost it would be down the back of the sofa at her mum's house, at very least, her mum would know where it was

Mhairi stood away from the easel, and retired to bed. The end to a rather strange Tuesday.

The Moggy Minor Traveller crept northwards along the motorway at a solid fifty miles per hour, its only occupant was Phillip (never Phil') Harrison. By dawn, Phillip would actually be in Glen Coe, at the end of a one way trip, with no intention of ever going back.

Phillip was the sort of person who only drove when he had to, he hated driving, more, he hated traffic, so it was without any real surprise that he'd set out from his home in Coventry, long after the rush hour had ended. At Midnight, he was passing through the Lake District and was making for Carlisle, as each minute passed the roads quietened, the hills became more frequent, and Phillip's heart felt glad.

Born, bred and living in Coventry, he'd been a leading light in the world of mountaineering and rock climbing. The Midlands were not the obvious place to express that talent, he needed rocks and mountains for that, but mere geographical-positioning never stopped him. Every second of his spare time was spent in the hills or mountains; whether it was in the Alps, or closer to home; whether it was summer or winter, he'd be climbing something; always suffering the journey to get there and get his fix. He became exceedingly good at what was, to most of his work colleagues, just a hobby. To Phillip though, it was his reason to exist.

Thin, bald, five-foot-seven and athletic, he changed down a cog to allow his over-burdened car to make the next hill. As the car crested, he changed back into fourth and relaxed slightly. His rheumy, grey eyes fixed stoically on the road ahead, and every now and then, he wiped away the excess moisture from them with a tissue that he kept, sat in his lap.

Phillip knew he was old, too old now for the shenanigans of his youth, his best days were well behind him. The doctor had knocked him for six when he'd told Phillip that it was inoperable, a death sentence with a too finite amount of time for an appeal to be heard. Brain tumor is not what you want to ever hear, coming from the lips of a doctor! Phillip accepted his lot in life and made plans, he'd packed his old car with everything he thought he might need, and everything that meant anything to him.

Packing, meant days of methodical stacking. The clothes and mountaineering kit were the least of it. He'd plied through piles of photographs and articles that he'd kept, going all the way back to before Edmund Hilary had even climbed Snowdon, let alone Everest, and Phillip had been there though not on Everest, unfortunately. The photographs would be gifted, at some point, to whomever expressed an interest in them. Everything was tidy, everything had its place, and given a few seconds, Phillip could lay his hands on any particular item, photograph or shoe, carabiner or sock. He had lived this way the whole of his bachelor life. He'd stood away from the packed car and admired the lowered rear suspension, wondering how it might affect the ride up north.

At Annandale Water motorway services at two in the morning, Phillip parked up and opened his flask for a well deserved brew. Devouring two cheese sandwiches and a few moments answering the call of nature would see him passed Glasgow. He looked at his watch and did a few mental calculations; reckoning on another five to six hours of travel time, he'd definitely have to stop again otherwise it would be too much. He got back into the car and pulled out a road map from the pocket in the door, tracing his route, he worked out where he thought he might stop, maybe even catch up on some sleep before finishing the journey. He started the engine again, left the service station and headed north on the M74.

Even at this early hour, the traffic into Glasgow was building. Phillip would avoid most of it by heading to Stirling before cutting back across country to pass through the Trossachs. He always came this way and rarely had he been held up for long, even through the small town of Callander. At Callander he'd find somewhere off the main road to stop and replenish his energy, probably get some fuel for the car too. She deserved it.

At sometime after five in the morning he parked the car in a small side street on the outskirts of the town, shut down the engine and closed his eyes for forty winks.

Feeling refreshed at seven, he set off again and completed the rest of the journey without any further stops. By nine in the morning he was driving down through the glen, surrounded by the majestic mountains he so loved; it was like coming home. He wiped away a tear and slowed the car as it descended Rannoch giving him more time to take in his surroundings. Phillip didn't care about the line of traffic behind him, they'd have to excuse him for being an old man in an old car. At a stately thirty miles-per-hour Phillip drove the glen with a great deal of respect. Those behind him would call it annoying, funereal respect; but Phillip entered Glencoe with dignity.

Phillip was to stay at the Ballachulish hotel, he'd managed to get a late room booking at a very reasonable rate, it was only a single occupancy room, with no real views from the windows but it included breakfast, and the option was there for him to take dinner there too. So it suited his purposes, and he had booked for an initial one weeks stay. After that he'd see how it went. His room wouldn't be ready until after lunch though, so for a while he had time to kill. He decided he might grab a breakfast at a small cafe on the old road through Glencoe, then walk off the drive with a bit of exploration, and generally re-attain his bearings.

Just an hour or so before Phillip had pulled up to rest in Callander, Grace, sleeping peacefully, entered a strange dream, like walking through an open doorway, but one with such colour and vivacity it eclipsed all of her dreams of late.

She walked the beach, not as Grace in her youth, but as the Grace she was now. Her movement was effortless, with no aches or pains, or any problem walking through the broken surface, littered with rocks and pools. In her night dress and in broad daylight she wandered unashamed and proud. Under her arm she held onto a box of intricate design. The box was made up of square shaped tubes each about a foot long, their square hollow profiles only large enough to contain a pencil or a biro in each one, but there were forty or fifty, bound together to make the whole box. As she walked, she lowered the front side of the device, and aimed it like a gun towards the path she felt inclined to follow, and suddenly, from the hollow tubes, minute marbles of ruby-red erupted out onto the beach; a myriad of sparkling, ember, rubies grew and littered her path.

Grace stepped onto them, barefoot, while the device spewed even more, covering every surface of her route forwards. The rubies glistened, and as each footfall made contact with them as she walked, those she trod on went out and turned to black momentarily, until her foot was lifted again to step upon the next. The blackened footprints slowly reassembled their ruby glow.

The ground beneath looked hot and sharp, but Grace appreciated the precious stones like a deep pile carpet beneath her feet, soft and luxuriant. Still the device rained more out onto the beach, until every inch of the shoreline in view was buried and smoothed by the lustrous red orbs.

She reached the very edge of the shore and looked out across the loch, the device she'd carried was no longer there. In her hand she now held a lit candle, flickering in the slight breeze whenever she moved. The day had turned to night in an instant, and she stood with her feet in the water of the loch. The water was warm and inviting and holding the candle out in front of her, she could see it was like glass. The flickering candle burned even more brightly, throwing out rays of light that formed a new path, straight across the loch towards the mountains on the far side.

Stepping onto the surface of the loch she followed the extended route now available to her, beckoning her, with no concern as to what lay beneath. Beneath her feet the depths shone like diamonds catching the sun, she glimpsed fish and kelp forests by the light she held. Continuing towards the far shore, the colours she saw in the water beneath her, radiated and throbbed, pulsing up from the seabed, purples, greens and blues in so many shades she couldn't count them, moved in wavelets becoming golden at her feet. She stopped walking just short of the far shoreline and turned back to face the way she'd come. On the now, new, distant shore a bright white light shone with such intensity that she had to shield her eyes from the glare, the whole shoreline glimmered red beneath it. She found herself transported towards it in a blink.

A chair was set before the light, that rose from the beach and pierced the night sky, and she sat. The candle became a golden mace as she sat upon a throne, and she was garbed in robes of satin and ermine, and upon her head she wore a jewel encrusted crown. The light diminished enough to see that there was something held within it, a figure from the depths of her dreams, the man, who knelt before her in loyal obeyance, and awaited her command. The figure didn't speak, just waited and Grace knew it would continue to wait.

Grace awoke, this time she stayed in bed. The cat jumped up, and curled up next to her. Grace reached out and stroked it, always thankful for its company.

She knew that it had never been Death she'd spoken to, all those years ago. But on that day, she had called out for death to take her, and the only one that had responded, was the voice in her head. Death and demons didn't exist. Of that, she was almost sure. There had to be another explanation, but she wasn't sure she wanted to find out what it was.

After a while Grace went back to sleep, cradling next to her the cat, who purred, pawed and nuzzled into her side.

At the time that Phillip awoke up in Callander, Miles opened his eyes, fully rested. He got dressed quietly and put the kettle on, leaving Julie asleep for just a few minutes more. A definite way to earn a few brownie points, waking her gently with a piping hot cup of tea. No dreams had woken him and no voices had made an appearance throughout the night, the dragon had kept his word and kept quiet.

When they'd both breakfasted they left their home and wandering across into Glencoe. The bus into Fort William would be along any moment, and they got to the bus shelter in good time to meet it. As the bus travelled following the shore line, Miles noted that the tide was in. The dragon would be completely submerged at present, it would be a lot later on today when he could be sitting on his raised rock in discussion with him, if indeed he got back before dark. The one thing Miles was certain of, although he could keep a tight rein on his fear in the daylight, he wasn't sure the same would apply in the pitch black of night. For now he was just happy to be watching the scenery unfold from the relative comfort of the bus.

In Fort William they alighted the bus near to the restaurant on the pier, and made their way to the High Street. Once there, they spent their time window shopping for the most part, until they got to the far end.

At the far end, outside a mountaineering shop, there stood a cable car suspended from a fixed pylon; this was to be the starting point for the actual shopping.

Wandering about shops with Julie was not on his favourite to-do list, especially clothes shops, but he grinned and bore the tedium of following her, going from one rack to another then back to the first rack again.

'What do you reckon to this?' she asked, holding an item against her body. Miles payed attention for the minimum amount of time, he thought, he'd get away with.

'Very nice, love.'

'Oh, I'm not sure. Is the colour right for me, Miles?' Miles nodded, knowing that Julie wouldn't take a blind bit of notice with what he said anyway.

Sometime he wished she'd come out with the classic. 'Does my bum look big in this?' And he'd deliver the well remembered lines. 'Your bum looks big in everything, dear!' But Julie was never going to ask that question. 'Pity.' he thought, and continued being led around the shop by the collar and on a short leash.

The small quantity of food shopping they had to do was available from one store. Miles elected to stand outside, almost forgetting himself. 'I'll wait here with the-.' he caught himself before he finished mentioning the dog that wasn't there. When Julie finally exited the store, Miles took the heavier of the two bags, the one that weighed heavier probably contained a bottle of whisky, so he felt he'd better guard that.

One of the next shops was a book shop. They both went in and busied themselves in totally separate sections, reading the titles, occasionally flipping a book to read the back cover. Julie liked books that were true life, as she put it. Miles always knew when she'd found a good one, tears would roll, as some unfortunate led their torturous life, before coming good and writing their story down, for Julie to read. Miles liked fiction, although he sometimes thought Julie's selection would be likely fiction, more than fact, anyway. He ended up buying two books, purportedly set in Scotland or on one of the Isles. Julie had a handful. Miles, dutifully, added the books to his burden and they took to the street again.

By lunchtime, everything they'd wanted to do, had been done. There was nothing left, but to find a pub with some decent food, and rest up for a while, before catching the bus back to Glencoe.

Adjacent to Glencoe Mountain Rescue's base, at the pedestrian-crossing, and heading towards her parents house, Mhairi witnessed the cortege that drove solemnly through the village, an old Morris Minor at the head, leading the procession. Perhaps forty cars and lorries, trapped behind the small car up front, breathed an audible sigh of relief, when the Minor turned off the main road to find somewhere to park. Mhairi could see the other drivers' looks of despair, as each vehicle passed her and accelerated away, at last.

After a cup of coffee, sat at the dining room table, with her mother, Mhairi divulged to her mother what was eating away at the back of her brain. 'Mum, this may sound like a weird thing to ask but- I had a chat with a couple of friends I met in the pub last night, and the subject centred around dragons, and-'

'So what do you want to know?' asked her mother, trying to make out that she had little time for such nonsense but happy to encourage her in whatever line she pursued.

'Something in the back of my mind, tells me, I know something about another creature that lived in the glen, but I've forgotten what?'

'Come with me dear.' she said, with a smile. Her mother rose from her chair, and made her way to the back door of the house, Mhairi followed. 'Look up there.' her mother pointed her finger up to the hills and out towards the west. Mhairi's eyes traced an imaginary line from the end of her mother's finger, towards Corrie Liath and the mountain it sat within, and she remembered.

'What's your new found interest in dragons about then?' her mother asked, happily, more overly because Mhairi had mentioned that special word, friends.

'It's just something, a fairy story, that I was trying to bring back to mind, that they don't know about.'

'You think it's a fairy story then?' her mother asked in a slightly admonishing tone.

'Well it's got to be, hasn't it?'

'Personally, I think that most fairy stories are bound in truth somewhere along the line, and I wouldn't be surprised if this one was too.'

'I wouldn't have put you down as the sort to believe in myths, Mum. You think there might have been a beithir then?'

'Mair', I think there might have been a something!'

Mhairi hated being called 'Mair' by anyone else, to rhyme with mare, but from her mother... totally acceptable. She walked over to the kettle and put it on for another coffee and her mother told her all about the beithir again.

Chapter 8

After the shopping was put away, and with still a couple of hours of daylight left, Miles wanted to test a theory.

'Fancy a bit of a walk?'

'Where to?' Julie answered

'Just along the front by the loch, maybe pop in to see the craft shop on the way round.'

Julie didn't mind the sound of it at all. The weather forecast was good for the rest of the day, but tomorrow, the wind would be getting up. Some storm with a ridiculous name, was apparently, battering Ireland at present, and it was on its way towards mainland Scotland.

They set off, and once across the River Coe, they took to the scrubland and skirted the loch, trying to avoid the roadside footpath as much as possible Eventually Miles led the way onto a beach, between larger boulders that protected the scrub. At a certain point he stopped and crouched down. Rummaging for his tobacco tin to roll a cigarette, Julie decided to spend a few minutes at the very edge of the loch, looking into its dank water for any signs of life, maybe the swish of a kelp frond in the current, or a sea anemone. Occasionally, she looked up to see if Miles had finished smoking, from her angle, she couldn't see that Miles was talking to himself. When the smoke signals stopped, she made her way back towards him. Miles stood, and they continued their walk along the shore.

Miles's theory was proven, he didn't know what it meant, but Julie was not privy to the dragon's conversation with him, or maybe, she couldn't hear his own mind speaking to itself. He'd actually not proven anything that he hadn't know before!

Guessing the approximate position of the shop, they eventually headed off the beach, and cut across the rough grassland, towards the road, fortunately, finding they were directly opposite the craft shop now, they crossed the main road and entered the white, rough-stone built shop. A small cafe formed the main part, with gifts and art pieces on display for purchase. Spending a short time perusing the wares, and after catching the eye of Mhairi, working at the back of the shop, they took a seat at a table and waited for service. Mhairi, who seemed keen to join them, stopped what she was doing, and approached them. They both ordered a piece of fruit cake and a coffee off her, and she disappeared to fetch them, bringing a third coffee for herself. Looking round the shop, it was easy to see why she also worked in the pub at this time of year; Miles and Julie, not exactly the greatest purchasers in the world, and Mhairi, and that was it.

'May I?' she asked, taking a seat with them. 'How was Fort William?'

Miles nodded a hello.'Not as good as it used to be.' he said. 'There seem to be a lot of closed down shops now, and the bar I wanted to go to, was closed, for renovation or some-such.'

'Which one was that?'

'The Grog and Gruel, we ended up in one of the bars opposite. It was still a nice meal.'

Julie interjected. 'It's the same everywhere, though, look at where we live, half the empty shops are turning into charity shops now.'

'I think it's a shame.' said Mhairi. 'We're all buying on-line these days, and the rates for a shop are phenomenal, it's no wonder they're closing down.'

'The streets look so jaded and scruffy, when half the shop fronts have boarded up windows, or the glass is smothered in Windolene.' said Miles, re-picturing the unkempt windows along the High street.

'A sign of the times.' said Mhairi. 'Any more thoughts on your dragon theory?' she asked keenly, and she seemed more smiley than usual.

'Haven't really thought about him.' Miles said, and suddenly prayed that no-one had noticed the 'him' part.

'I have.' she said, excitedly. 'I was wracking my brains, trying to think of where I've heard the myth of a dragon in the glen, then I realised it wasn't a dragon I was searching for, so I popped in to see my mum and she reminded me this morning. We have a sort of dragon here, or used to, at any rate, if you believe in that sort of thing.'

Miles coughed through his coffee. 'Here?'

'It's a fairytale or a part of folklore. I'll try and get this right, but I was told it when I was a kid, and mum told me the story again today. Excuse any mistakes I make but the gist of it is this...'

'Of course. Go on.' prompted Julie.

'Well, once upon a time, there was a beithir, that's a sort of a dragon, or serpent, it doesn't have wings and it doesn't breathe fire, it does rip people to shreds however. Anyway, it lived in Coire Leath. If you look up to the mountain above Ballachulish, it's the corrie thats to the right of that huge gash that cleaves the mountain. You can see it better past the Ballachulish hotel. The dragon used to attack the villagers and anybody who happened by it. Anyone that met it would be stung or killed by it. If you luckily only got stung, there was one cure, you had to get to the loch, and immerse yourself in the water, before the beithir could get down to the same water. If you didn't make it, you'd die. I think most people who met it, were ripped apart though. The only way to kill it was to remove its head. But if you managed to do that that, without being killed, you then, somehow, had to destroy the head, otherwise it would just come back.' Mhairi took a sip of her coffee, before continuing. 'I had a quick look on the internet, and they appear to be a water monster or spirit. But they are nothing like the Loch Ness monster. From what I gather, they are a spirit, rather than an actual beast, they come classified as being one of the fuathan, and the fuath seem to be able to change their form. The funny thing is, that the name, beithir, also means a wild beast, or lightning, it didn't occur to me at first, but the mountain above is called Beinn a' Bheithir, in English it would be the 'mountain of the thunderbolt', or the 'mountain of the lightning', but, I suppose it could also be the 'mountain of the dragon'. After I realised that I got a map out and looked out the other things in the area too. There is a 'Dragon Rock' at Ballachulish, and the golf course there, is the 'Dragon's Tooth Golf Course', I mentioned them before. There seem to be quite a few other dragon related names in the area as well.'

'This beithir, is it a living, breathing, creature then?' Julie asked.

'Not necessarily. It's a spirit being, one of the fuathan, it can shape shift. I suppose it could be anything.

Julie asked.'What does fuath or fuathan actually mean?'

'Literally, I think it means hate.'

'Could it be inanimate then?' Miles wanted to know.

'I suppose it could be.' Mhairi answered.

'So, Miles isn't as stupid as he looks then.' said Julie, grinning from ear to ear like a Cheshire cat. 'One up to me.' she thought, and Miles knew that she'd got one over him. Miles, however, he'd had his tentative idea reinforced though, so he sat there quietly, feeling vindicated.

They drank their coffees and ate their cake, Miles spoke, deep in thought. 'Just going for a ciggy, won't be long.' He left the cafe, reaching for his tin.

Julie was looking around at the art upon the walls. 'Which pieces are yours, Mhairi?' Mhairi pointed at a few of the larger pieces that lined the walls. Julie took them in, noticing they were generally what she'd describe as being modern art, but very different, more bizarre, and darker than the images that fitted with her interpretation of the genre. Mhairi had used blocks of vivid colour. Close up, they were randomly scattered, the brush marks went every which way, and deep. Overlapping paint layers produced a second colour, overpainted again to give a third, a fourth, or even a fifth colour. The more colour applied, the darker the overall effect and every bit of the canvas was smothered. Julie stood up and backed away from one particular painting she looked upon, and as she retreated from it, the daubs and random thrashes of paint, formed a whole. She squinted her eyes slightly, and the thick soupy mess in close-up, vanished, revealing an incredible landscape, and it virtually came to life, bursting from the framed canvas.

Mhairi smiled, as she watched Julie's expression change, from one of incomprehension to one of revelation. 'They're pretty hard to get right. I spend a lot of time squinting, and standing down the end of the hallway when I'm painting them.'

'How long do they take?'

'That one you're looking at, took about a week. It was one of the quicker ones, one of the ones that went right.'

'They're fantastic!' Julie exclaimed. 'Do you sell many?'

'Not as many as I'd like. They take a bit of getting used to, and you need a huge house to put them in for the best effect. I tend to sell more when I get gallery space, that way you can stand well back and see what it is.' Julie walked up close to the painting, and looked at the ticketed price, the label said seven-hundred and fifty pounds. She took a noticeable intake of breath and turned her head away minutely. 'That's another reason I don't sell many.'

'If I had that amount of money to spend, I'd buy it.' Mhairi smiled at her, understanding and knowing the price.

'Where did you get the idea from to paint like this?' Julie asked, moving back, away from the painting again.

'It sort of developed over time. I used to paint normal landscapes, but they weren't very special, then I got these,' she indicated her tattoos by holding her arms out for Julie to see. 'and things just developed from there.'

How come?'

'Well, you know what the tattoos cover, I know you do, but what they cover, is the close up image you can see. The further away you get, the nicer that image becomes! It was a concept that took ages to achieve.' Mhairi's tone of voice lowered. 'You've never asked me about my burns! Why?'

'It wasn't my place to.' Julie turned and looked at Mhairi's arms and hands. 'It's always been you, we wanted to talk to, not you're arms.'

'Is that what you *really* thought, Julie?' Mhairi stressed the 'really'.

Julie took her seat at the small table again before answering. 'No, I didn't, I disliked your tattoos and thought they were a mess, and you've got such a pretty face, Mhairi. I just thought you were one of those rough kids, the sort that thinks it's a sign of being tough. It was a shock when I realised they were there to hide your burns.'

'So why didn't you back away like everyone else does?'

'Because- you're interesting, Mhairi. Miles wanted to hear your story about the girl in the village, and, we listened, and, I like you, Mhairi. My initial response was based upon not seeing the burns, just the tattoos. I was more annoyed at Miles, for wanting to bring you into the conversation. Lets face it, when Miles gets going, talking about some weird shit, you don't want innocent bystanders involved. The good thing about Miles though, is that he had seen your burns through the ink, as he put it, and Miles doesn't judge anyone on first impression. Maybe I do, a bit. The burns are yours, if you wanted to talk about them you would, and as I said, it's not my place to talk about something, that you might want to keep private.'

'Thank you for that, Julie.'

'Thank you for what?

'Just for being honest with me.' After a short thoughtful pause, she added. 'Miles is quite strange, isn't he? I can't work him out.'

'Me neither, and I've been married to him for thirty-eight years.' They both started laughing.

'What is this fascination with dragons he has?' Where has that come from?'

'I have no idea. It's a totally new one on me, he's never mentioned them in his life before.' Miles opened the door and re-entered the cafe.

'Talk of the devil.' said Mhairi, and both women fell about laughing again.

'Am I missing something?' They both shook their heads in denial, trying to keep their faces glued with an expression of seriousness, and they both failed miserably. One snigger set the other one off and Miles just stood there, wondering what the hell had happened while he'd been out.

'I'm going to lock up in a few minutes, will you be going to the pub tonight?'

Miles nodded. 'We hadn't thought to, but we may as well. Are you working there tonight?' Miles had thought that he might like to take in the pub on his walk, but he didn't want to appear too keen. Now he'd got an excuse to go. 'I love it when a plan comes together.' he thought. He looked towards Julie and she tutted. He smiled back at her, giving her his best, puppy-dog-eyes.

'No, I only do a couple of nights a week, they always seem to be the quieter nights, Tuesdays and Sundays. If you give me a minute, we can pop along now, they're open all day.'

Mhairi removed the dirty crockery from the table taking it into the small kitchen at the back of the shop, she placed it in the sink. 'I'll sort that in the morning.' she said, grabbing her coat. All three of them left the shop and walked down the road to the Gathering.

Outside it had grown icy cold, and dark, it was still quite early, but it was obviously that time when everyone shut up shop, made their way home, or headed to the pub. The traffic on the road had increased, and the way it moved, intoned an urgency to the journeys in motion. Looking through the windscreens of the cars that passed them, as the three of them made their way to the pub, stern faces, on a mission, looked straight ahead at the road. The only thing on their minds, was the end of the journey, not the route it took them.

The path they trod was treacherous, and they slipped and slid their way along, supporting each other to ascend the sheet-ice, slight rise in the pavement, just outside the pub.

Inside the Gathering, early customers were settling in to having a few drinks and order a meal. Miles and Julie weren't the only holiday-makers in town, that was certain, but accompanied by Mhairi, they felt even less like the tourists that they were.

They found a vacant table against one of the windows, that looked out into the dark and up towards the glen, and took seats; Mhairi and Julie on one side, a pile of coats and Miles on the other.

'What are we having then?' Miles asked.

'I'll get these.' said Mhairi quickly. 'Besides, I think I've sold a painting today.' She looked at Julie's face and started giggling. Julie met her look and started giggling too.

'Bitch!'

'What is it with you two?'

Mhairi answered. 'Just having some fun.'

'Strange idea of fun.' he said. 'Tell you what, we'll put it all on a tab and sort it out later.' Miles took their order and went to the bar.

'While he's gone, I'll tell you about my burns.' Mhairi wanted to, she'd thought long and hard about the telling, and Julie was so approachable, so she set her stall out, and told Julie about what had happened when she was a child. Julie made faces that amplified her reaction to the pain. The pain that Mhairi, must have gone through. When she finished her abbreviated story, she said. 'I don't tell many people what happened, Julie, you're one of the few I felt I could tell.'

'Why me?'

'You just seem a bit cooler than what I expected you to be. I don't know, easier some how.'

'But I'm old enough to be your mother!'

'It's not age that matters, you can't choose your friends based on age.'

'Well if you did, you'd have to have a questionnaire ready. How old are you? Too old! Goodbye.' They both laughed again.

Miles returned with the drinks, and the conversation transitioned to the history of the glen.

'We went up to see the monument in commemoration to James Stewart.' he said. 'Seems so sad that he was innocent. The monument inscription says he died, but he was killed there!'

Mhairi bowed her head a subtle amount. 'A lot of really bad things have happened around here. Next to the massacre, that's probably one of the worst.'

'Do you know what the story was?' Julie asked.

'All I know is it concerned the killing of someone called Red Fox, his real name was Colin Campbell and he was a factor for lands that had been forfeited by the Stewart clan. Even though James had an alibi for his whereabouts when Colin was killed, the jury found him guilty, and he was hung where the monument is. I think the jury he had consisted of eleven Campbells, out of the fifteen man jury. I think the judge was a Campbell too. It was all a bit lop-sided and unfair.'

Miles asked, 'What happened after he'd been hung?'

'He stayed there on a gibbet for eighteen months.'

'Has he ever been pardoned for the crime?

'Not as far as I'm aware, but what would be the point of that?'

Miles and Julie stopped in their tracks for a few seconds, taking in the enormity that an innocent man could have been tried, convicted and died that way. Until Julie, whose thoughts had strayed, broke the silence. 'Wasn't the Glencoe massacre caused by a Campbell too?'

'It was, sort of, but under very different circumstances.'

'In what way?' she asked.

'He was called Campbell but he was under orders, not really from his clan. He was just the man that everyone remembers, the one that had to carry out the orders, as far as I can remember from school.'

Julie accepted the coincidence of name, but wanted to know more. 'So who gave him the orders?'

'I'm not too sure, it was all very political. The MacDonalds were not well liked and they were tricked, they were slaughtered by the very people they were feeding and giving shelter to. Something by law that they had to do. All in all it was down to the government at the time, they'd throw a few disliked people to the wall, so the rest might fall back in line. That's the way I see it.'

'Politicians are a law unto themselves!' Miles said. 'No-one can really believe that they do it for the good of the people, most, are only there to fuel their self worth, and make a lot of money.'

'Let's not go off on politics, Miles. You have your ideas, but Mhairi's might be totally different.'

'It's all right Julie, I don't mind. Out of all the things you're not meant to discuss in public, we seem to be doing quite well at ticking them off. Money, religion and politics. It's a good job I like you two.'

Miles picked up his whisky glass and took a sip. While he savoured the Aberlour's spicy start and gentle punch to the back of his throat a commotion, towards the entrance, caught his attention, he swallowed. The barman on duty rushed passed their table, a look of concern on his face. Mhairi stood up and duteously followed him, a company girl even on her day off. When Mhairi came rushing passed them again and towards the bar, Miles asked. 'Is everything alright?'

'Some-one's slipped over on the steps, they're hurt pretty bad.'

Miles, who had taken a first aid course at work, rose to his feet, and made his way to the door, hoping his meagre knowledge might be of assistance, while Mhairi picked up the phone, at the bar and dialled for an ambulance.

Outside, it was bitterly cold. Lying at the bottom of the steps that led to the decking in front of the entrance door, an unconscious, elderly man was being stood over by the barman. The barman, who seemed to be in a state of panic, looked at Miles. 'I don't know what to do, we're calling an ambulance.'

Miles re-entered the pub, and picked up the pile of coats, that had sat on the chair next to his. Outside again, he carefully negotiated the steps, down to the man lying there. Lying on his back, with his upper torso still raked upon the two stairs, and his legs on the gravel path, not moving. Crouching next to him, Miles checked him for signs of life and any injuries that were obviously present. Finding the man to be breathing, Miles breathed a sigh of relief. With a gash to his forehead, and no sign of any further bleeding, or certain broken bones, Miles placed the coats he had recovered over the man, draping them like blankets to try and keep him warmer.

The barman spoke. 'Can we move him, he looks so uncomfortable?'

'No we can't! We don't know what injuries he might have that we can't see and we don't know how he's fallen. Can you find some more things that might keep him warm? And get me some clean serviettes!' The barman stepped over and passed the man leaving Miles, crouching down beside the casualty. As the door opened, Miles heard the hubbub from within, and looking up at the windows that lined the front of the building, he could see the faces of the onlookers, warm inside and not wanting to get involved outside, not on a night like this. Mhairi came outside, bringing with her some blanket throws, She passed him some paper napkins and crouched down next to him. Mhairi placed the throws over and around the man, carefully avoiding moving him, and Miles applied the napkins to stem the flow of the bleeding wound.

'The ambulance is on it's way. Neil's gone back behind the bar, he looked pretty shaken, thought it was for the best he stay there.'

'How long?'

'Hopefully fairly soon, the stations only there, as long as there's an ambulance still on stand-by.' She pointed across the road.

'What's Julie doing?'

'She's fine, she told me she didn't want to get in the way, so she's staying by the phone, just in case.'

'Good.'

Beneath the blankets and coats, there were signs that the man was slowly coming to. Miles put his hand out and touched the man gently and re-assuringly on his shoulder. 'Try not to move, mate, you've had a fall. What's your name?'

The man's eyes flickered open, and he looked up to Miles. 'Phillip.' he said.

'Well, Phillip, the ambulance is on its way, it shouldn't be long.'

'I'm okay, I don't need an ambulance, if I could just-' Phillip tried to move, but a searing pain across his head forced him to give up on that idea. That, and Miles hand, encouraging him to stay down in a semi-reclined position.

'Is anyone with you, Phillip?'

'No, I'm here on my own.'

'Is there anyone we can call for you?' Mhairi asked.

'No, there isn't.' Both Miles and Mhairi perceived a hint of sadness in Phillip's voice. Keeping Phillip occupied, through talking to him and keeping his mind off the discomfort he must surely be in, angled across the treads of the steps, it wasn't long before the ambulance arrived, all sirens and blue flashing lights. Miles looked up to the windows, and if there were a few faces there before, everyone was there now, but not Julie. Blues and two's, in Miles's opinion, had the result of bringing out the worst in people. Rubber neckers!

The ambulance guys took over after a chat with Miles, and Miles and Mhairi got back into the warmth of the restaurant. Miles walked over to Julie, and placed their coats back onto the chair, but started to put his own on. 'I'm going to go with them.' he said sullenly. 'Phillip's on his own here, he needs someone.' Julie nodded and Miles gave her a hug.

'Mhairi and I will be okay. Just give me a ring and let me know what's happening, won't you?'

'I will, I promise.'

The stretcher with Phillip loaded upon it, was placed into the back of the ambulance, and after a brief few words with the ambulance crew, Miles stepped aboard to accompany Phillip in to Fort William.

Chapter 9

The ambulance they rode in swayed violently as it sped along the road towards the hospital in the town. Miles gripped the cot-sides of Phillip's stretcher, as yet another tight corner was careered through. Looking out of the darkened windows, Miles watched the reflections of the blue lights that flashed about them. Phillip was fixed in place by a spinal board and staring straight up at the roof of the ambulance. On one arm he wore a blood pressure cuff, and the paramedic with them spent the time monitoring Phillip's condition, inflating and deflating the cuff and writing notes.

Once they reached the hospital, Miles was parted from Phillip, who was rushed straight through to be assessed, and Miles was left to wait in the pastel-blue waiting room. After what seemed an eternity to him, a nurse came out and located him.

'Are you the gentleman that came in with Phillip Harrison?'

Miles looked about, before realising she meant him. 'Yes, I am, how is he?'

'Are you a relative?' She looked at him questioningly. Miles had told the paramedic that he was Phillip's son. He'd felt he had to, Phillip was scared, and had asked Miles to go with him and the only way he could be sure he'd be able to go, was to lie. Now he thought it would serve him better to be prudent, and to tell the truth.

'No.' he said regretfully. 'I was just there with him, and he didn't appear to have any one else to call on, so I thought I'd better stay with him.' She looked at him knowingly, and raised an admonitory eyebrow.

'You found him then?' she asked, assessing his answers very carefully.

'No, I was one of the first people to get to him, and I just assessed what I could see and protected him from the cold, while we waited for the ambulance.'

The nurse took in what he had said, and decided how much of what she knew she should divulge to Miles.

'You didn't need to lie to the paramedic. But, I suppose you felt it best to come in with Phillip, being as he was in your charge. I can't tell you much, but, he seems to be a tough old bird. Other than a cut to his head, he seems to have come off quiet lightly from his fall. He's had an X-ray, and they're stitching up the cut as we speak.'

'Will he be free to leave, when that's done?' Miles asked.

'I think he'll be staying in tonight, under observation, but he should be able to leave tomorrow. I'll call you when you can come through and see him, if you like.'

'That would be great.'

Miles waited for the nurse's return, reading a dog-eared magazine that seemed to contain a lot of adverts for stair-lifts and walk-in baths; of absolutely no interest to Miles, but it gave him something to do while he waited. When the nurse returned he'd already started to read the signs and information bulletins scattered about the walls of the waiting room, he'd even learned how to

Hibiscrub. Thankfully, she called him to follow her, and he was led into a small side room. Phillip was sat upright on a bed, wearing the regulation night-gown that the hospital had provided, and five stereostrip sutures held the cut on his fore-head together. He smiled as Miles entered the room and the nurse left them.

'Thank you for what you did. I don't even know your name.'

'It's Miles, and don't mention it, it was nothing.' Miles stepped towards the bed's side and proffered his hand to shake Phillip's, Phillip gratefully took it.

'It was something.' he said. 'I'm a complete stranger to you, yet you came with me to make sure I was alright. Not many would do that! Most people I know would have run a mile.'

Miles hated being revered, and desperately wanted to just talk, pass the time, until he knew what was happening. 'Really, it was nothing. What have the doctors said?'

'They were a bit concerned after the X-rays. Apparently they found a mass and it got them in a proper fluster, I can tell you.' Phillip held an infectious grin and it grew wider.

'What did they find, then?'

'I'm going to be blunt now so don't go all sorrowful on me, will you!'

'What-.'

'I've got a tumour, and it's not a good one, so, I'm up here on my final world tour before-. Well, you get my drift!'

Miles swallowed hard, he'd never heard someone speak so pragmatically, about a life threatening illness before. He didn't know what to say.

Phillip broke the silence. 'Struck me like that at first, then I just decided to get on with it.' his smile never left his face. 'Then bugger me, the day I arrive, I end up slipping on some bloody ice, trying to get a pint.'

Miles put two and two together. 'That's why the nurse questioned me!'

'What did she ask you?'

'She just seemed a bit cagey with me, when I asked after you. I think she realised straight off that I wasn't you're son.'

'My son! Is that what you told them?' Phillip laughed heartily then involuntarily regretted it and palmed his throbbing head. 'I suppose she can't say anything without my permission.' Phillip mused. 'I knew I'd got a tumour a few weeks back, but last week I was told it had gone too far. There's not a lot they can do for me.'

'What are you're plans now?' Miles wanted to know.

'Looks like I'm stuck in here, on my best behaviour. I might get an early release, if I'm a good boy.' Phillip's grin arrived and never faltered. It was like a ray of sunshine on a bleak day.

'Better keep smiling then!' said Miles.

'I always do, son. I always do! All being well I'll be back in Ballachulish tomorrow. This is my ticket out of here.' He pointed at his face and Miles knew Phillip wasn't going to have a problem getting out of there; his pearly whites on display were better than hypnotism.

Miles and Phillip talked for a while longer, Miles eager to find out what made Phillip such a happy, contented person given that he'd had such bad news recently, and that he now found himself, in this hospital.

After an hour with Phillip, Miles was encouraged to go home by the nurse. One last hand-shake, a quick telephone call, and he was outside heading towards the taxi rank and his way back to Invercoe.

At just after eleven-thirty the taxi took him on to the site, and after a few directions, dropped him in front of the van. Miles payed and got out, he walked the last few feet to the door, opened it, and found Julie and Mhairi inside, slightly the worse for wear judging by the giggling and the two empty wine bottles displayed on the table.

'Had a good night, girls?'

'How's Phillip?' Julie slurred, concerned and trying to hide her obvious state of drunkenness.

'He's fine, he'll have a bit of a headache tomorrow, but otherwise he's doing great.'

'Come on, sit down, and tell us all about it.' She passed him a glass and hoicked an un-opened bottle of Talisker down from the cupboard. Miles took the bottle and split the foil top, removed the cork stopper and poured a very large water of life.

'I need this!' he stated, admiring the scent that emanated the glass, a scent that so reminded him of the sea, before finally, taking a large glug to satisfy his taste-buds and throat.

Miles told them about Phillip and about how he had never stopped smiling. He saved telling them about Phillip's condition. If Phillip wanted them to know about the brain tumour he'd have to tell them himself. Both Mhairi and Julie listened intently to Miles as he mentioned how he thought the nurses might really want to discharge Phillip at their earliest convenience; Phillip was likely to be big trouble with his wicked schoolboy ways; they wanted to know more and Miles told them what he felt he was entitled to tell them.

'It was approaching one in the morning, when Mhairi tipsily took to her feet, with the intention of heading home. Julie watched her, and started to laugh.

'Miles, smy darling?' she managed to say, and Mhairi started laughing too. 'You've got to walk Mhairi home, being ash you're the only one who can still walk!'

Miles knew an order when he heard one and there was no way he'd refuse Julie's command. He helped Mhairi into her coat, put on his own, and helped her out of the motorhome and away from the warmth. The freezing air caught his lungs as he inhaled it and initiated a stiffening of his body. The ground, it appeared, didn't like his foot-falls. He held onto Mhairi's arm, supposedly, to support her progress, but she seemed to be in better shape. She hadn't sobered up much and she trod the frozen footpaths in a relaxed, confident manner seemingly more sure-footed than Miles. Miles just skated this way and that, supported by the four-wheel-drive, Mhairi.

After fifteen minutes, they'd reached Mhairi's house. Slightly less drunk now, she turned to face him before she headed into the house.

'You've not told us the complete truth, have you Miles?'

Miles was at a loss. What hadn't he mentioned about Phillip? 'What about?'

'I've read the series of books you've been reading, and nowhere does it mention a dragon.' She looked him straight in the eyes. 'There's something going on, isn't there? Wouldn't you like to share it?' Miles held her gaze. There was something so astute within those eyes. In fact, there was something astute about all of the women he'd met recently. He didn't want to lie to Mhairi, but there was no way he could tell her what was really going on. Not yet.

'Yes I lied, but I can't tell you why. Just take it, for the moment, that there is something-.' he hunted for the right word and failed to find it. 'I'm just too scared to say anything at the moment. I need to sort it out in my head and then I'll tell you, both of you.'

'Is it bad?'

'No, it's not bad, it's just complicated. Give me a day or two and I'll have it all sorted.'

'Miles,' She reached out and touched his hand. 'If you need any help, just ask me!'

'I will Mhairi, I promise.'

As she turned to walk away and enter the house Miles had one further question, but never got to ask it, It was with regard the fuath but it would wait.

A part of him so wanted to enter the house with Mhairi, to unburden himself with this beautiful young woman, but he remained faithful and loyal to Julie, he'd probably be reading the signs wrong anyway, he always did. Mhairi was becoming a really good friend.

'Julie knows there's something going on, she's worried about you, but she's just too scared to ask what it is! Please speak to her, Miles!' Mhairi said as she walked away from him

Numbed by his thoughts and the biting cold, the slide back home was over in a flash. And slide he did, like a ten year old child doing his best to attain a rate of speed before sliding along the ice, one foot in front of the other and knees bent. He toppled less, he made quicker progress and it felt great. To be a child again!

Upon Miles's return, the bed was made and Julie was lying in it, wrapped in the duvet and reading. Miles undressed and got in next to her, determined to tell her some of what was going on. In his mind, though, he couldn't find a way to start off so he elected to leave it until the morning. He leaned across Julie, and kissed her goodnight on the cheek, turned away and closed his eyes. So much coursed through his mind. He imagined tens of alternative starts to the conversation he needed to have. None of them had an easy start, none of them had an easy outcome.

Eventually, with nothing further forthcoming, Julie put down her book and switched off the light, without a murmur. She stared into the blackness and inwardly worried.

It was still dark outside when the storm hit. Ferocious winds scorched across Loch Leven from the direction of the bridge, and hit the campsite head on. The trees that lined the shore edge amplified each gust with their roars of defiance. Then a second later, the motorhome was buffeted left and right as the wind deflected off the mountains, and steered around obstacles in its path to ultimately try and un-seat the motorhome from its pitch.

The storm carried hail, and fired marbles onto the fibre-glass roof above them. Julia and Miles sat up in their bed and opened the blinds to witness the wrath beating the ground outside. Inside the sound of thunderous hammering doubled, as the hail bounced to re-hit the roof again. The skylights vibrated and shook in the blasts of wind, and the van bucked like a bronco trying to lose a rodeo rider.

As the hail headed further up the glen to be replaced by a softer downpour of stair-rod rain, Miles lay out his cards.

'I'm sorry I've been a bit off recently, and I know I haven't told you the complete truth.'

'What is it, love?'

'Just, I'm having some issues and they've been worrying me-. More, scaring the crap out of me, actually.'

'Just tell me, I can't do anything if you don't tell me.'

'I'm hearing a voice in my head! Well I think I am anyway.'

'How do you mean? You're either hearing it or you're not. You must know the difference?'

'It's not as simple as that. I'm not sure if the voice I'm hearing is from inside me or from an external source. I'm having conversations with the voice I hear, and the voice is too real. It's got emotions and feelings that aren't mine.' Julie listened intently and worried.

'Is it telling you to do something? I don't know-, telling you to harm yourself or something?'

'No!' He answered, sounding almost surprised by the question. 'It's quite caring and gentle. We just talk and-well, nothing, we just talk. He wants to talk to me, and I seem to want to talk to him.'

'When you say him, do you mean the dragon?'

'How did you know it was a dragon? I've not told you that.'

'It's not too hard to work out, Miles, with all your weird questions and your fixation on them at the moment. With everything you've said recently, it's starting to make sense.'

'Well not to me it isn't.

'Is the dragon speaking to you now?'

'Well, no.'

'Where do you speak to the dragon?'

'On the beach, near to Ballachulish.'

'Have you seen the dragon?'

'I'm not sure. What I have seen, is a hulk of an old boat, and the voice tells me that it's him. But I'm still unsure, I still think it might be all coming from me.'

'So, you hear a voice in your head and it tells you it's a dragon. Why would a voice you hear in your head tell you that, if it was coming from inside your own head? God, that sounds so confusing!' Julie looked into the distance and thought for a moment. Miles let her. 'Does it matter whether it's inside you, or a real dragon talking inside your head?'

'That's the way I've played it so far. If I am going mad because I'm hearing this voice, it doesn't really matter which way it's happening, does it?'

'You're not going mad, Miles!' she said soothingly. 'So how do you prove which one it is?' Miles considered the question for quite a few seconds before answering.

'If it's from an external source, say the dragon, then I suppose I need it to tell me something I couldn't possibly know. Then all I've got to do, is prove the truth of what I've been told. Sounds so easy. If it turns out not to be the truth, then I must have made it up myself.'

'It sounds like a plan, but what if it's something you've just forgotten?'

'Then it has to be a fact relating to something or someone I have never known, seen or met.' Both Julie and Miles thought for a while.

Julie asked. 'How do you speak to the voice?'

'I don't really need to, it seems to be able to read my thoughts and it extracts the information from them. But I didn't like that, so I made a deal that it could only respond if I mouthed the words, and it seems easier to deal with now.'

'In your heart of hearts, what would you prefer it to be, you or the dragon?'

'The dragon. If it's the dragon or the beithir, that Mhairi told us about, I suppose a part of me will think I am not going quite as mad. It's the lesser of the two evils' Julie mulled over something Miles had said earlier.

'You said it was a he. Why do you think it's a he?'

'The voice I hear is male.'

'But one of your theories, when you first started talking about dragons, is that they just appeared on earth, not from an egg or born, like we are. And when they die, they are the first and the last, from a lineage of one. Doesn't that mean they are sexless?'

'I can't answer that, all I know is, it sounds like a male voice I'm hearing.'

Miles continued to tell her everything he could remember, about his conversations upon the beach, afterwards he felt like a great weight had been lifted from his shoulders. Julie just sat and listened and as he completed his story, she put her arm around his shoulders, nestled into his neck and pulled him in closer. Together they both listened to the wind, the rain and the storm, as it battered their motorhome on the shores of Loch Leven.

Chapter 10

The wind outside raged and the windows in their frames rattled but denied the storm access to the small bedroom where Grace slept soundly.

From her vantage point high above the loch, on an inaccessible, narrow ledge towards the top of Gleann a' Chaolais, the eagle looked down upon her world. Feathers that ruffled in the breeze rising the corrie, did not disturb the majestic bird's concentrated appraisal, as it located minuscule movements within the blades of grass hundreds of feet below. An ability, not even questioned, could discern between movement caused by the wind and that caused by a tiny mouse. To a human's eye, in that same place, the grassy slopes would lay motionless and featureless, just a single page torn from a book of maps.

Grace left the ledge with a single step. Her wings flared outwards and with not a flap she was gliding across the walls of the corrie, rising gracefully on the updraft. Turning about at the end of a rather exhilarating, soaring climb, she gained even more height using slow, sweeping turns, spiralling way above the mountain. At a point she reckoned was high enough, she set out towards the loch. The mathematics of vectors, wind speed, velocity and weight factors not even a thought, she just could. Sailing across the sky with a total contempt for effort, using only minimal, natural alterations to the dynamics of her broad, golden wings. And all the time, she watched the ground.

Every rock and every pebble on the beach below, even from so far up, was like she held it in her hand, to be able to scrutinize each blemish and hollow that every stone carried.

A person, clad in coloured clothing, similar to the hues and tints of the shoreline, stood out like a shining beacon against a grey backdrop. Camouflage was of little use when the viewer was an eagle. A perceptible shift out of phase with the surroundings as the subject moved, was all she needed, and Grace relished in the magnificence of unerring sight and of flight itself.

Heading inland she cut a swathe through the air, her flightpath cleared of any other bird by her just being there. The sides of the mountains, as she careered like a jet across the crags, sideways on, flashed passed. She banked and then altered her flight plan to take in the other side of the valley, to swoop at those flanks, almost touching the massif as she plough-turned away from it, and back onto a new found rising air-flow that carried her heavenwards.

At the very end of her undemanding flight, she chose her spot to settle and alighted onto a ledge on the steep sides of Meall Dearg. Surveying *her* glen and all it contained, the warm sun on *her* feathers, she was the queen of her domain.

Out to the west she was aware of a herd of deer grazing the flanks of the mountain. A large stag, keeping look-out, stood majestically proud a few yards above them and in a fraction of the time it had taken to realise that the deer were there, Grace was that stag. Transported from the queen of the skies to the monarch of the glen in the twinkling of an eye. A noise below, further down the slope, startled Grace, climbers or walkers? She knew not, but people, and she took to her hooves, the rest of the herd alongside and following.

Streams cascading the slope, runnels and rivers in the making, were leapt in a single carefree bound; the uneven sides of the mountain, that rock strewn facade, flowed beneath her like it was as smooth a surface as the road that wend it's way downwards towards the men folk and the village.

Once Grace was certain that enough distance had been put between her and the disturbance that caused the flight, she stopped in a large patch of bracken to resume her watch. The other deer stopped too. Unless you were a very short distance away, they all would have disappeared from view.

Grace awakened later than normal that morning, having had one of the best nights sleep she could remember in a long time. With the vivid dream so fresh in her mind, she got out of bed with a smile on her face. She especially liked the part where she ran as a stag. Life was always better running.

Downstairs, with the cat sat on her lap and purring, she revisited the two dreams she'd had in the last two days. 'Why now?' she whispered out loud to the cat, as it bunted her hand. 'And why has *it* called my name?' Remembering three nights ago. 'These dreams are too-surreal, so what is the significance of them?' Grace had never believed that dreams held a hidden meaning or that they should signify something, she was far too cynical for that, but now she wasn't so sure.

The cat turned its attention away from bunting her still hand because it was not achieving the, yearned for, rubbing of its cheeks or the attention it sought. It started kneading at her cardigan instead with an even louder purr to accompany the mauling. Grace ignored the clawing animal.

Grace had no doubt that the dreams were instigated by the thing she'd encountered on the beach, the 'black-shiny' thing she'd called Death, but she could not make head nor tail of what they meant. Pushing the cat gently off her lap and transferring it onto the cushion beside her, the shell-shocked cat started washing and preening itself. Certainly aware that she wan't clean enough for Grace's attention or maybe just being self indulgent. Grace went through into the kitchen and prepared herself breakfast.

Outside, the rain slashed at the windows but Grace felt safe in the centrally heated house, warm and dry and somewhat removed from the vicious weather. She pondered on the two dreams and their possible meanings, but nothing made sense. The only thing that was damned obvious to her, was that she couldn't remember one dream she'd ever had, prior to these two.

Frisky, the cat, was pushed out of the back door after breakfast, much to the cat's distaste and clawed remonstrations. Grace watched it dive for cover under the bushes that bordered her small garden. After a time of watching and waiting from behind the closed door through the rain splattered glass, a time that Grace thought was enough, she opened the back door again and called out the cat's name. In a flurry of wet bedraggled fur, the pissed-off cat flew past her and headed upstairs to seek sanctuary, away from the sadistic Grace.

Grace walked through into the sitting room, switched on the radio and settled into an easy chair. She barely listened to the drivel coming from the radio's speaker, content to just look out at the weather and think.

No doubt on Monday she'd once again catch the bus and head into Fort William for her weekly outing. She'd nod her thank-you to Ronnie; She'd sit alone in a small cafe, cradling a slowly drunken cup of tea before getting back onto the bus and returning home. This was her life, the way it had been for a number of years now, that didn't mean she enjoyed it. The more she thought about it, the less she found she was enjoying life. Drivel on the radio and a television that was a total waste of time. The only thing that kept her going was her devotion to Frisky, she looked after him and Frisky gave her something back, a reason to continue. And even the cat had done a runner from her now.

Grace felt like she was ready for a break, a long, long break, the eternal rest type of break. But the dreams held something in store for her and if they continued, maybe she would continue too.

Chapter 11

As daylight surfaced and scratched its way through the un-curtained windows of their motorhome, Miles and Julie lay entwined together, both fully awake. Julie didn't want to let go of Miles, as she felt it was her time to protect him. Eventually though, discomfort crept in and they both got out of bed to start the day. After a coffee and some breakfast and with the rain still slashing down, Miles knew he needed to face the dragon.

'I need to go to the beach, strike while the iron's hot.' he said, as if he knew what he was doing.

'Will he talk to me?' Julia asked.

'You couldn't hear him yesterday when I spoke to him. So I doubt he can speak to you at all.' Miles instantly regretted the way the words sounded as they passed his lips, in one fell swoop he had shunned Julie again.

'Is it just that you don't want me there?' she said icily. Miles couldn't think of a better time to have Julie with him, but a part of him recognised how one sided and utterly beyond belief this would appear to her; him having a nice chat with himself or the dragon, Julie just watching him mouth words, silently, for however long it took.

'There's not much point you coming along, if you're there watching It'll probably look even worse than it is already. I think I'd better go alone.'

'As you wish, but you had better come back to me as my Miles!'

'Why don't you go and see Mhairi when the weather improves a bit? She seems to know more than I've told her and she's worried too.'

'Just take your phone with you and let me know what's happening, Miles.'

Miles, dressed for the weather, walked away from the campsite and Julie. He splashed his way through the puddles that lay upon the bridge over the river, and headed towards answers to his questions, he hoped. When he got to the beach the tide was still covering the rock he normally sat upon, and water lapped most of the boat's bones. The tide was in the throes of ebbing but prevented him from taking his usual place before the wreck. He stayed amongst the bigger boulders at the high tide mark, and found a seat that afforded some shelter from the horizontal rain that didn't fall, but swiped at any exposed skin put in its path.

'Dragon?' he spoke out loud towards the only part of the wreck he could see, the bow, tipping its nose towards the sky as if trying to breath, like a seal snorkeling in an open sea.

'Hello Miles, I'm glad you're here.' Miles shook away the image.

'Dragon, can you hear me if I just mouth the words from here?'

'Miles, I could hear you when you were talking to Julie this morning, I heard you when you were speaking to Phillip last night in the hospital, I can hear you wherever you are, within a reasonable distance anyway.' Miles sat stunned by the relevance of what the dragon said, it was paramount to an intrusion into his private life.'

'But, but that's not fair,' he stuttered. 'Those are private things, you might have understood them incorrectly and- well it's just not right.'

'Miles, I can not shut this off, I never could, not since I found you when you woke me from my sleep in your time of need. We are connected Miles, and that connection can not be broken readily.'

'But we had a deal, that you'd only take into account what I mouthed.'

'And that's exactly what I've done. I've promised to only act upon your mouthed information, but I still know everything as you think it and I can't do much about that. I'm sorry Miles, I can't switch this *knowing* off. Your thoughts are like my own now.'

'So none of my thoughts are private anymore?'

'They never have been, but even the negative ones, where I'm concerned, are like water off a ducks back to me. They have no bearing on what I think based on those thoughts, nor how I feel about you. You might think I'm a bastard, and nevertheless I won't be offended or misconstrue what you thought. I'm simply not able to Miles. Every thought is as much my own as it is yours. You remember what you wanted to say to your father after he had died and you visited him and sat beside his open coffin at the undertakers?'

'Errr, Yes.'

'You wanted to call him a bastard for certain things he'd done in his life that directly affected your life.'

'I remember.' Miles didn't want to remember. In the end he'd never spoken those words, he chose others to say, words with less impact, then kissed his cold father goodbye. 'What's it got to do with this?'

'Your father would have forgiven you those words even if he had been alive to hear them. He'd have forgiven you because he loved you. He also wouldn't have misconstrued them, maybe you should have told him earlier what your true feelings were, maybe things would have worked out different for you.'

'What the hell has my father got to do with you?' Miles spat.

'I'm sorry, Miles, I'm just trying to point out that you can think anything you want, I won't misconstrue what you mean and if you are totally honest in what you say, it might be easier for you to move forwards.'

'Easier! Fucking easier! No need to read my lips there then!'

'Miles? Take a moment and think. What I've said proves I am in your mind and I can't stop that. I can read you like a book and I can't stop that either. This is about your acceptance of those facts.'

'But thoughts! They're all random at times.'

'I think that might be the way your mind is wired, Miles. You work through associations, and even the tiniest ones have a bearing on what you're thinking and how your thoughts change.'

Miles remained silent for a few minutes, almost expecting the voice in his head to start humming an inane tune to pass the time while he was waiting for Miles to speak again, maybe do a bit of whistling. He smiled at the thought and he slowly calmed down.

He bought to view his thoughts the day he'd made the, so called, deal with the dragon. A knight on a white horse with a lance sounded pretty good about now. 'Did you see my thoughts of a dragon being slain, when we tested if you could read my lips?'

'Of course I did, but it bore no relation to what we went on to talk about, you asked me what it was like being a dragon. The images you think and the questions you think seem unconnected and I've read you in just the way you wanted to be read. Anyway I knew it was a way to test me, but why should I have responded to that? It would have made you feel uncomfortable and that's the last thing I wanted. I want you to feel safe, I want to help you, and maybe you might help me in return.' Miles wondered how he might be able to help the dragon, and could come up with no feasible scenarios, whatsoever, that fitted the bill. The dragon didn't choose to mention those fleeting thoughts and waited until Miles was ready to go again.

Miles formulated a new question, the most important question he could come up with.

'I need proof, that you are a dragon and that I am talking to you, and, that I am *not,* definitely *not,* having this conversation with myself!'

'So how do you want to proceed then, Miles?'

'Well you already know the answer to that one, don't you? I'd be wasting my breath telling you, wouldn't I? You know what I spoke about, with my wife this morning!' The rain in conjunction with Miles's disappointment at finding that his thoughts were- so open to view added an edge to his delivery.

'Yes I do Miles, but I made a promise to you, just so you'd feel better talking to me, and I'll try not to break that promise again, not until you give me permission to do so. So what is our way forward?' The voice in Miles's head sounded stronger than before, within, it carried an air of exasperation. 'We need to move on Miles, what is it you want me to do?'

Miles asked in the way he'd virtually practiced it. 'Tell me something I can't possibly know?' and added. 'That I will be able to prove as being true.'

'I'll tell you the story of Grace then, but it's a very long story, and to get to the point of something you could prove to be true, I need you to hear the whole story.'

'Why do I need to hear the whole story?'

'Because otherwise, you will misunderstand the reasons for what I have said and done. You will also form conclusions that aren't true, concerning Grace, and I can't have that. I need you to be there'

'How long will it take?'

'Everything I want to tell you, may take a few hours if we talk as we are now. But there is a quicker way to experience it all and I don't think you'll like it.'

'And that is?' Miles had an inkling as to what it might be and he wasn't looking forward to the feeling of being that powerless, to have the dragon taking control of his mind. He might never let go, Miles might be lost forever, and he'd promised Julie he'd return as 'her Miles'.

'I need to place the story into your mind in the same way that you might dream it. It's the quickest and only way.'

'Will it hurt?'

'Do dreams hurt, Miles?'

Miles thought about his dreams for a few moments. Bad ones had certainly woken him up in a cold sweat at times, and made him bury his head under the duvet, but they had never physically harmed him. The good dreams he'd experienced were the ones you didn't want to wake from, if you did, you tried to re-immerse yourself back into them, always with limited, or no success though.

'If I allow you to place this dream into my head, will I remember it all?' Miles's dreams generally didn't stay in his mind for too long, bits of them fell away and the remnants that were left were undecipherable; like trying to read a newspaper that is slowly burning, the page gradually disappears and each paragraph becomes incomplete. After time, there are not even sentences that make sense, and finally the words and letters vanish, never to be read again.

'Yes, this one will be like a memory, and you will be there, witnessing it happening, being a part of it and controlling it, just like in a dream but one that you won't forget.'

Miles had to make up his mind, finally accepting that this would happen, but fleeting thoughts flew in fast.

'Will I be a character in the dream?'

'Will I be able to pull out out the dream?'

'Will I be able to control the dream?'

'Will it scare me?'

'Will I be conscious of being here?'

'Will I be conscious of you being here or there?'

'Will I still feel the rain?'

The dragon spoke loudly in his mind. 'Miles, I will break my promise to you because this is very important. Only you can answer those questions, and only after you've gone through it. No-one has ever told *me* what happens.'

'You've done this before then?'

'Everyone I've ever been with has received information in this way, and it never harmed them.'

'How can you be sure?'

'Because the information I'm going to give you, is about someone who's still living her life here. And one day soon, I hope, you will meet her on my behalf, then she can tell you.'

Miles accepted the inevitability of his situation and conceded to the wishes of the dragon. A part of him still persisted in the belief that he was alone, and talking to himself, this portion of his brain could accept, more readily, the attack he was about to undergo. Because, after all, his own thoughts couldn't cause any harm to him. Or could they?

'So how will this go? Do I need to close my eyes or anything?'

The answer from the voice never came.

Miles found himself totally immersed in an impenetrable blackness. Only the sound of the rain, as it pelted his waterproof coat, crept through the murk to be heard. Miles felt that even that light drumming seemed to be receding, either that, or he was just getting used to ignoring it. His eyes located brown splodges within the murk, that swam randomly across the dark overall picture. He tried to follow their direction, and found himself attempting to count how many worm-like apparitions filled his vision, as they squirmed their way towards the peripherals. Yellow and Blue streaks of lightning began flashing, horizontally, between the slowly settling patches of brown, that now merely pulsated like jellyfish. Miles, mesmerised by the new colours, tried controlling the rate of their departure, trying to focus on each individual strand as it flew away. Light blue started sneaking in, to mute and soften the sharp edges of the electric storm, and the whole picture merged and transitioned into a cloudless sky. The rain had stopped, the sun was out, though he couldn't feel its heat, he couldn't feel his wet coat either, he was just there. A spectator.

Looking about him, he could tell he hadn't moved, he was still wedged between two rocks seeking the shelter they held from the- non-rain. Everything was much the same as before, but for the colours, more vivid now, and not a hint of the drabness that smothered and choked his view of a while ago, an unimportant forgotten view. This was the real view of that day. The sea was a lot further away than he might have remembered, and how long had he been here? Wasn't a question that entered his head.

Miles stood up easily, and smoothly flowed towards the boat halfway down the beach. Red paint, he hadn't noticed before, bubbled and cracked with age, plastered most of the hull side planking. The boat was more a boat than a wreck but Miles had never seen it in any other way, it had always been like this.

A girl with blonde hair was running towards him, distress like an aura, emanated from her, he could feel it and he knew why. He wanted to cradle her and tell her everything would be alright, hug her until the pain evaporated, but he couldn't move. A barrier like thick glass restricted him and his urge to run towards her, he felt helpless but he was soulful and thoughtful. After a while she prayed to be taken by death and the barrier released. There was an intense feeling of deep love for the little girl. A love that eclipsed even the love of a parent, and he reassured her in her mind. Miles was both there, viewing and assessing, but also the girl, listening and talking. He gave counsel and in return he received it. Everything that had happened to Grace was as much his memory as it was hers. He felt everything and knew everything. He traipsed through his new memories, her new memories, her old ones were his too. He had become a god! But with it he was certain that neither Grace, nor him, were the play things of the gods nor actual gods. Without them, the dragon and death would not exist, could not exist. You can't have the one without the other, both were as important as the other, both a side of the coin.

Now he felt he wasn't even Miles, Miles didn't exist, Grace didn't exist, there was only one thing that lived upon that beach. A being that was neither male nor female, and a creature of such complexity that it existed in essence only, it was all and it was nothing. It was death and it was life, it was the dragon and it was the beithir and a part of him and a part of Grace, and that part was the only thing there. Everywhere, everything was one, every part, every person, every being whether life or inanimate, was one. Grace, Miles, the rocks, the sky, beithir, dragon, boat, the sea, all a part of one thing. Existence. Something ancient, something good. And Miles pulled away and understood, everything. Revelation.

The sound of rain ruined the dream, it pattered and thrummed, and Miles shuddered to life. Cold seeped into his skin and he struggled to control the shivering. He rubbed at his soaked arms, through his coat, to try and force more blood through his system, got to his feet and stamped the lethargy of his body away.

'Miles, are you alright?' The dragon's voice eased into his mind, full of concern.

'I'm fine, just cold.' Miles started walking round in circles, suddenly realising he was stood knee-deep in seawater. He moved away from the dragon towards dry land, trying to use some energy that might generate some warmth. The dream hadn't faded or even been jaded, it was as if he'd lived a proportion of Grace's life. He'd been there to witness her thoughts and musings, he hadn't misunderstood any of the randomness that goes to make up the coherent patterns of a real thought, he'd seen it all in vivid reality, in pictures, written and using every sense available to her. Coming back to the now, he knew he'd seen so much more. Miles wondered how all of this information might lead to it being proved.

'May I step in there and answer? Without you mouthing that pertinent thought.' the dragon said in his mind, without even disturbing the train of thought he considered.

'It can do no harm now.' Miles answered softly in his mind, without moving his lips, accepting and warming to the idea.

'Grace won't come to me, she won't answer my call to her because she's scared of the repercussions. Grace went to hell and back after she first spoke to me, and I didn't deal with her very well, you know that. I need her to be happy, I need to put things right. I need you to be my voice. If I can get Grace to see you, will you do that for me?'

Miles mulled over the words and couldn't refuse the request, given what he knew now. He wondered how it would be accomplished, getting Grace to meet him.

'In much the same way as you have now experienced.' the dragon said. 'Through a dream!'

Miles nodded and walked away towards the road. Looking at his watch, he worked out the figures and checked the date, he had only been on the beach for barely a quarter of an hour, yet it felt like months.

'I told you it was the quickest way!' a smiley voice said from within.

Chapter 12

Hanging his saturated coat up to dry over the door to the motorhome's bathroom, and his leggings threaded through the bannister rail that aided stepping up into the motorhome; Miles relished in the heat that the small fan heater, sat upon the floor, gave out. He located dry clothes and fetched his slippers from beside the bench settee on his side of the van, sitting down to remove his walking boots and change. Julie stared at him for any sign that he had been altered in some small way. She saw none.

Miles looked up from his white, wrinkled fingers and their remote battle with double-tied, wet laces, and looked Julie squarely and firmly in the eyes. 'I love you.' he said, and he had never meant it more than at this moment. He scanned through the cliched references in the past where he'd written or said, 'I love you more today than I did yesterday,' and he doubted they were true, but today, they applied to the umpteenth degree.

'What happened?' Julie asked with bemused concern, almost determining that he was drunk.

Miles told her what had occurred on the beach, to the best of his ability, he tried to explain the complexities of being a part of it all, of being actually the subject and the master of all that had happened. In his head it was so lucid, but his words couldn't convey the knowledge of a portion of Grace's life, that had taken weeks, in fact years, for her to live. All of it had been crammed into a fraction of the time it had taken her, to live that life. He knew, because he had been a part of everything that had happened between Grace and the dragon and more besides, but Miles found it hard to express the emotions and the love he'd felt. Words didn't' cover those feelings adequately. He did his level best to purvey it all to Julie, but he knew his explanations were somewhat lacking; he could talk for weeks, months, years and he'd only chip the surface of what he knew.

When he finished his abridged version he felt elated, happy, happy beyond any happiness he'd had for a long time. He reached out with both hands taking Julie's hands into his. And he couldn't explain why, he just needed to. It was like he was trying to use telepathy to talk to Julie's inner self. He settled for the comfort she gave him, just by being with him.

'What happens next, Miles?'

'I suppose we wait and see if the dragon succeeds in convincing Grace, then we'll know whether he's really real.'

'It sounds like you already believe he's real.'

Miles smiled. 'It does, doesn't it?'

They sat talking for a while until Miles's phone rang. Answering the call confirmed that Phillip was out of the hospital, and back at his hotel. They chatted for a few minutes, with Miles repeating the same mantra, that refuted he was a key reason Phillip was doing so well, or that Phillip's circumstances might be very different if it weren't for Miles, and he repeatedly said, 'You don't need to do that, Phillip'.

When he shut down the call, Julie questioned. 'Well?'

'Phillip's out of hospital.' he said.

'Well I guessed that. What's he doing?'

'He wants to buy us all a meal at the pub this evening.'

'And you said, no?'

'He wouldn't take *no* for an answer, he insisted, so it looks like we're going. He wants you to get in touch with Mhairi, she's invited too.'

'I don't have her number, I never thought to ask for it.'

'After lunch, we'd better go and find her then.'

With lunch out of the way, Miles eased into his wet and repellent waterproofs with a look of agony upon his face. The way they now clung to his skin because of the cold, clammy moisture that had equalized onto both the inside, and the outside of the garments, was repulsive. Once he got moving, they'd start working again, forcing the frigid liquid away from his body. He hoped.

The rain had abated for a while as they stepped from the van to head into the village. Now it came in abrupt squalls, driven by the persistent wind that howled about them as they walked. The ice of the previous night was gone, thawed by the warmer westerly storm. Out on the loch, the storm had fetched up waves like a herd of wild white-horses, that galloped to the shore.

'Nature was definitely in a foul mood today,' thought Miles, as they passed the small school on their route. In the playground, the children were playing in defiance to the weather, all were dressed in waterproofs, some were racing about in a game of tag, others played hopscotch, but all of them seemed totally unaware of the tempest.

To Miles it brought back memories of his junior school. On a day like today, they'd all be prisoners to the classroom, none of them would have been allowed outside. He supposed that the main thing that had changed was the advent of new, fully waterproof and breathable materials. When Miles was at school, he had his Sunday best coat that was brown and woollen, or his blue anorak. That item was made of nylon, but with so much patterned stitching that it allowed the thermal layer to soak up any moisture. The padding becoming a sodden clump inside the lining of the coat. Nowadays the kids wore brightly coloured, membrane cloths and stayed dry and warm.

Where most people seem to think that today's children are a part of the snowflake generation, Miles considered these kids to be the total opposite, the children that disproved the point. Maybe in a few years they'd expect everything placed upon a plate for them, maybe they'll moan at the slightest niggle or consider themselves the unfortunate ones, but at this time, these children were the future adventurers and inventors.

Outside the craft shop cum cafe, an old parked-up Morris Minor caught Miles's attention as they approached, he smiled to himself as he noted how the rear suspension appeared to be struggling just to keep itself raised a few meagre inches away from the road. Inside the cafe, sat at a small table was the beaming face of Phillip, with Mhairi sat opposite. Phillip's brow, resplendent with sutures and a burgeoning bruise that was going to cover half his forehead given time.

Phillip stood up as Julie entered. 'And who's this delightful young woman?' he asked. 'Surely, she must be your daughter, Miles?'

'I see you've not lost your sense of humour then, Phillip.' Miles replied and instantly regretted it as Julie's hand gave him a playful slap on his arm. 'This is Julie. And that there is Phillip!' Phillip's grin couldn't possibly get any wider, graciously he reached forward and took Julies hand to kiss it before moving around the table to pull a vacant chair out from under the table, and invited Julie to sit.

'Julie you've met Mhairi, my little saviour, have you?'

'It was her we came to see, to tell her about your generous offer of a meal. You really don't need to, Phillip.'

'I insist. It'll be my pleasure to see you all there tonight.'

'That's what Miles said.'

'I'll get my own chair then, Phillip. Shall I?' Miles announced, with a hint of sarcasm but delivered with jest.

Phillip pointed at his cut. 'Well I've not been well!' Miles quickly looked away from Phillip's grin as the paradox hit home. 'Less of that, Miles! This is a happy occasion.' Mhairi looked towards Miles like she was wearing a question mark on her brow, and Phillip noticed the look she gave him.

'Better get this out in the open then, I suppose. The elephant in the room. The thing is, Mhairi, I've got a tumour and, as I've already told Miles, there's not much that can be done for me. So, here I am with my new friends and I don't want to be treated like I'm fragile, or I'm going to peg it at any moment. I just want to enjoy what's left. So there you go, we don't discuss this again. Okay?'

Miles raised his eyes from the table and nodded his agreement, while Julie reached a hand out towards Mhairi, who now wept silently and openly.

'Come on girl! Get a grip, otherwise I'll have to tell you some more stories about mountaineering.' he beamed.

Miles's face brightened. He saw a chance to lighten the mood 'Is that what you were talking about?'

Phillip nodded. 'It seems I may have bored Mhairi with a few anecdotes from my past.'

'Understandable.' Julie said with a wry smile, imagining Miles's similar tales.

'Some of them are bloody good stories. Pardon my French!'

'I'm sure they are, but maybe you should tell them to Miles, he's more into that sort of thing.' Mhairi nodded a little too enthusiastically at Julie's suggestion.

'It's not that I don't find them interesting,' Mhairi said, 'it's just that I don't know what half of what you've been saying means. I wouldn't know a prusik from an extender if I fell over them.'

'Point taken, Mhairi, I'll not tell you anymore climbing stories.' His smile, even in defeat, never wavered. 'I could still tell you the story about the time I woke up next to a sheep lying in the sleeping-bag next to me in my tent.' he continued with a naughty schoolboy grin.

'Maybe too much information there.' said Miles, before Phillip could get going. 'Maybe save that one for later.'

After hearing the story of Phillip's journey up to Scotland, and that of his unfortunate brush with a set of stairs. Miles and Julie told the gathered throng about the reasons they visited the area year in year out, the scenery, the mountains and lochs, the people and lastly, Julie spoke of Skip; now it was Mhairi's turn to take Julie's hand with a compassionate squeeze.

Trying to brighten the sombre mood that they'd now fallen into, Phillip pointed at the artwork on the walls and initialised a new topic. Mhairi discussed her art, and Phillip took great interest in her ideas. To Miles he appeared to be a bit of an aficionado on the subject. Phillip knew the right terms and words that described the pieces on display. Unlike Miles's own appraisals of artwork that would either contain the words 'crap' or 'not bad'. Whether Phillip liked them or not was hard to confirm, with his permanently affixed smile, Phillip was just so charismatic and full of the joys of life.

Eventually the subject matter turned to the one Miles had been dreading would surface, but he felt powerless to stop it. A tentative, subtle exploration pulled the focus away from Miles, however, and placed it firmly into Mhairi's lap, and all done through her paintings or at least, a new direction to explore and depict upon canvas.

When she laid out the bare bones of *her* idea for a series of beithir inspired works, Miles still wasn't sure whether it was real or a ploy. Whilst re-visiting the myth of the beithir for the benefit of Phillip, Miles still didn't know, but he listened politely and attentively. One word Mhairi hadn't mentioned before stood out, and it bore into him like a razor-sharp talon, malevolent! The beithir was a malevolent, spirit creature, in line with all of the fuathan.

Troubled by the new information that Miles had picked out about the creature, he withdrew from any involvement in the conversation for a while. Popping outside to grab a cigarette and trying, at the same time, to stay sheltered from the wind and rain, he searched for clues that would confirm or contradict the possibility that the dragon was indeed evil. Wracking his brains, he could not justify that it was truly malevolent, but perhaps the dragon would prove otherwise and turn on him in the future. But on what grounds? The dragon had admitted to an error of judgement regarding Grace, but that didn't make it evil, that made him- more human. So, was the dragon endowed with human traits? What did he know about the dragon anyway? But then what did he know about how the human brain works?

The more he thought, the less he knew. It was like the optical illusion whereby you climb the stairs, but you never reach the top. Even though on paper, you can trace that all of the treads go up, they still eventually meet up with the one's you've just ascended. Miles had ascertained information that had led him to a certain level of understanding, he'd taken one more step, and that had just led him back around again. The only thing he knew for certain, was that for him, the dragon was the lesser of two evils. But if he thought about that too long, he'd change his mind. He couldn't work out how he knew that everything in existence was connected, he just knew it, and if he thought about that too long, he'd go batty. Miles stubbed out his cigarette and opened the door to the cafe.

After Phillip had been fully briefed on all aspects of the beithir, and Miles had re-taken his seat at the small table, Phillip threw a few ideas their way, in support of the idea that mythological creatures may have existed in some form or another. He also brought to the table, a host of other mythological creatures, that may, or may not, have lived alongside man at some time in the past, and he came up with compelling theories that linked the creatures, on a worldwide level. Through nature, the elements, and unexplained phenomenon. With some deep consideration, Phillip tabled motions to be discussed, ripped apart and re-assembled. Mhairi, Julie and Phillip became key members of 'the mythological creature' section of the X Files. All that was needed to complete the picture, some other-worldly black and white photographs and the dramatic echoey music.

Miles managed to stay a little remote, and to not upset the debate by stating something that might bring it all back down on him. He thought back to that morning and suddenly remembered that the dragon might be hearing all of this too. He found out his tin and lighter and went for another smoke, leaving the debate society in full session.

'Can you hear me, Dragon?' He thought, mouthing the words silently as he pulled a cigarette paper from its cardboard sleeve.

'Yes I can, Miles.' The clear voice caused Miles to turn about quickly to check that no-one else had heard, and then he settled a bit as he realised how private this all was. It was only him. And it might only be him, until the alternative was proven.

'Have you heard everything that's been said today, that I've heard?'

'Yes.'

S J WARD

'Are you disappointed by what I've been saying or with any aspect of what we're talking about?'

'There's no need to worry on that score, Miles. I hear everything you think, and after all this time of hearing certain peoples thoughts, I have a pretty good idea how their brain formulates what is important. I'm neither disappointed nor heartened by what is being said, I'm not wired to work like that. Anyway, you all sound like you're having a fine afternoon, Are *you* not, Miles?'

Miles placed some tobacco onto the thin paper and started to roll the paper around it. 'It's been a great afternoon, and yes, I am enjoying it, but with some concerns. How come you don't just speak to me throughout the day, if you are listening?'

'That's easy to answer. You'd probably go mad if I incessantly spoke to you. Imagine my voice in your head and you couldn't shut it out at all. It wouldn't be nice, would it?'

Licking down the gummed-band on the paper, Miles sealed the cigarette and continued rolling it to loosen the tobacco to the required feel. 'No, I see what you mean. But can I ask you questions at any time I like?'

'Of course you can, Miles. Have you anything particular in mind now?'

'Might you be the beithir that we've been talking about?'

'There's no doubt it bears a striking resemblance to me, given what Mhairi has said. So I must be the beithir. I still prefer dragon though and I think that sits with you better.'

'So if you are a beithir, and a beithir is one of the fuathan, then are you malevolent?' Miles lit his cigarette and took a draw on it, shocked by how easy it had been to pose a question that reeked of negativity.

'That information, Miles, is a supposition, it's not based upon the whole story. I have my failings just like you do, If you think back to some of your actions, might they not also be regarded as being malevolent?'

'I suppose.'

'Miles, cast your mind back to what you did when you were young and naive, you made mistakes, does anybody bring them to mind now? They could, because someone will be around to remember them still, in your short lifespan. With me, I have lived such a long time and I have made mistakes too. I try to put them to rights, as you do. Maybe one mistake I made, was passed down through generations of your kind and became- distorted or exaggerated, if you will. If I had ceased to be, at the same time as the victim of my mistake, then perhaps that mistake would have been forgotten about, but I'm not that fortunate. Maybe! On the other hand, you likened your experiences of earlier, to be that of a god. If a god made a mistake, surely that would be paramount in everybody's minds thereafter. He could be considered to be malevolent based on one event or one mistake.'

Miles pictured the memorial to James Stewart and the words beneath it. 'For a crime of which he was not guilty, then?'

'Not really, Miles. I'm not saying I was innocent. I'm sure James Stewart made mistakes along the way, but what happened to him was a miscarriage of justice. I just have to accept that there are misconceptions carried by time that haunt me.'

Miles smiled. 'So even you are haunted then?'

'We all are in one way or another, Miles, but for me time is not a healer. You'd have thought that by existing for such a long time, it would get easier.' The dragon's voice tailed away.

Miles thought of the vision he'd had of Grace. 'Was Grace guilty of a crime in some way? he asked.

'No Miles, Grace was totally innocent in all she did and said, she was just young. It was my fault entirely, what happened to her.'

'You said you'd speak to her in much the same way I'd experienced, through a dream. Was what I experienced, really, just a dream?'

'There's no such thing as 'just a dream', Miles. A dream is as vital a part of life as a reality, it's all down to interpretation. Might not this chat we're having be interpreted as a dream or is it a reality?'

'I don't know. I think I do, one moment, then I'm not sure what's real or not, the next.'

'That's exactly what I think, Miles. Only with me, one decade I am sure it's a dream and the next I'm certain it's a reality. I've given up trying to differentiate between them. May I suggest you do the same.'

Miles finished his cigarette and re-entered the cafe to take a more active role in the debate at hand, turning it around at a convenient moment to discuss reality and dreams.

Chapter 13

Grace had never remembered any of her dreams since before she left the glen for Glasgow. Since then, her dreams, by the time breakfast was over, had always had a knack of evaporating away. It didn't matter how hard she tried, every single aspect of them just vanished and could never be recalled.

The dreams of the last two nights, though, were something very different to those of the past. These were gifts, she was beginning to believe. They wore the hallmark of having come from the thing on the beach, the thing she'd called Death. As to the reason behind them, she could not imagine, but the visions lay indelibly etched into her mind, and though they were of the pleasant sort, she was frightened of the implications. The thing wanted her to do something or act on something, of that she was sure. Yes, it was doing it in a gentle manner that caused little concern at present, but what if that changed? She knew the influence it could exert on her, it had clouded her mind once, but then again, she had been a child then, and she'd misinterpreted the meanings of what the thing had told her.

On the other hand, having these visions was nice. She'd been placed upon a pedestal and she felt revered, much in the same way, she felt, she had revered Death. So what could be so important, that he contact her now and give her these dreams?

Ronnie was at the wheel of the bus parked outside her house, as Grace walked towards it, she could see she was to be the only passenger. Not a whiff of a breeze played about her and the air was as warm as her duvet, the sun sat just right and didn't cause her to squint, or strain her eyes to see. Everything she witnessed was just pristine, the bus was shiny and new and Ronnie was an immaculately dressed adonis. He welcomed her aboard and escorted her to a special seat, right in the centre of the bus, with a three-hundred and sixty-degree panoramic view of the surroundings. Not a smear on the impossibly transparent glass, would impair her vision.

The bus pulled away and floated serenely down the road towards Glencoe. As it passed by bus stops with awaiting passengers, it did not slow or stop, nor did those waiting even realise the passage of the bus going by. Before the narrowed bridge over the River Coe, the bus turned right into the campsite, the horizontal red and white barrier raised, timed perfectly with the bus's un-slowed arrival. It stopped and Grace didn't need telling that this was her destination. She got up from her seat and exited the vehicle. The bus vanished, it just ceased to be, naturally.

Near to the entrance she had just passed through, a small herd of red deer grazed the lush, green grass. She walked towards them and they didn't scatter or run, as she expected these skittish, shy creatures to, but they raised their heads in recognition, then bowed them in her direction. Able to walk up to the nearest deer, Grace stroked the side of its face, from a juvenile velvet antler down across the coarse fur towards its nose. Its eyes didn't have that startled look in them, the deer regarded Grace appreciatively and lovingly.

She moved away and the deer resumed their grazing. Out to the west, in the distance, she could see the bridge across the loch, beyond, the mother of all sunsets. Within the hedge bound confines of the campsite, her eyes came to rest on the one occupying vehicle. It didn't even register in her mind that camping pods and permanent caravans usually belonged here, she'd seen them from the bus once a week for years. Today, there was only one motorhome. The motorhome sat within the one bit of ground that was gravelled, the rest of the site was completely grassed, not even a road led to the area it sat in, and no tyre marks explained how it got here, but that didn't cause Grace any concern. The van shone.

As she watched, a man opened the door to the van from the inside and stepped out. He was followed by a woman, and together they walked towards and stopped in front of her, Grace didn't recognise either of them.

In the voice she had heard a thousand times before, the man spoke in the same wrong voice. 'Hello Grace, would you care for a dram?' He held out a tot of whisky he'd just poured from a bottle of malt he suddenly held, into a cut-crystal glass that just appeared, and offered it to her. She took it cautiously. 'My name is Miles,' he continued, 'and this is Julie.' All three of them now held a glass of the same design containing whisky, and it seemed so unimportant as to how it had happened or where the bottle had gone.

Miles raised his glass towards Grace, 'Slànte mhath,' and she raised her glass to her lips and tasted the whisky, and it was more divine than she ever remembered a whisky tasting before. Miles and Julie joined her in savouring the nectar. A border collie ran across from out of nowhere and sat loyally at Grace's feet, encouraging with its perceptive brown eyes, a stroke of its thick collar fur. Grace knelt beside the dog and fussed his coat'

'That's Skip.' Miles said with difficulty, fighting back the emotions, but with a pride and honesty that Grace instantly recognised. And she could tell by the tears that welled up in Miles's eyes, that Skip was so loved, but so lost to him. She looked at the eyes of Julie and saw those same watery signs.

Even though Grace heard everything that was said, those few words, overlaid with the voice of the thing on the beach and the way she heard it, she couldn't help but notice how easily she had fallen in line. She was enjoying her dream to the fullest extent, she felt warm and contented, yet she couldn't explain why. The man and woman exchanged glances with each other, looking back towards Grace, she knew that there was more they wanted to say, but they didn't or couldn't. They went back inside the motorhome with Skip trailing after them and Grace was left alone again. She worked out that she didn't like the feeling of being alone anymore, and she knew she was craving for the company of someone, anyone.

The bus arrived at the stop she was stood at, in the centre of the campsite. The door hissed open, the bus knelt and she stepped aboard. Being driven back the way she had come, floating along on the smoothest of roads, and taking in the beauty all around her, it stopped outside of her house and she emerged into the night. The daylight had gone, and with nothing more to do she went inside and upstairs to bed. Looking down she found she still held the glass, and it still contained some whisky. She drained the remnants of the glass, put it aside and fell to sleep.

At her regular time, Grace woke up and desperately searched for the glass that she had placed on her bedside cabinet, but it was no longer there. 'Just a vision then!' she said out loud and her voice sounded full of disappointment.

She reviewed the contents of the vision in her mind. It had been the strangest of the dreams, in that it hadn't placed her in a totally improbable scenario. A lot of it was impossible, yes, she knew that, but this one involved a physical thing she would never have thought possible to dream of. The motorhome.

She knew the campsite and how it was laid out with its ranks and rows, roads criss-crossing the site to link the hard-standing or grass-standing areas, and all of the electricity points to service each van. None of them were there. The deer too, were absent from the site, the occasional single deer, it had to be said, got onto the site at times, until it found it would be better off back amongst the trees and on the hillsides. So it was an idealistic view she'd seen, but she couldn't shake the feeling that it meant something.

After breakfast she made up her mind to go and see the campsite first hand, the campsite didn't pose a threat to her, it was far enough away from her fears as not to matter. The bus was ready to go at nine-thirty and the twenty minute journey was nothing like the one in the vision. She stayed on the bus as it passed the site and she alighted just before the junction with the main road in Glencoe. She could have got off earlier and closer to the campsite, but she wanted the view from the bus as it drove by, she'd need to test the waters first. There was nothing out of the ordinary to see through the windows of the bus.

Walking slowly, coat flapping in the wind that still assaulted the glen, she followed the footpath to the bridge. As she came up to the entrance she looked inside, uncertain that she wanted to continue, but there it was, the barrier, just like she'd seen it. She followed the road in and saw the statues of two deer that guarded the entrance, planted in a raised floral border. Maybe these were the ones from her dream, but these were concrete and she had never seen them before, of that she was sure. Encouraged to go in further she started to look at the variety of caravans, pods and motorhomes that were scattered throughout the field.

She could negate the pods and the caravans from her search, and that left about four or five motorhomes of varying size and type. She walked the roadways through the site towards the centre, to prove, in her mind, the one she had seen in her dream was not there.

The first two motorhomes were in the wrong place, far to close to the amenity building to be right. But the third, almost in the centre of the field, towards the front and above the loch, with a windscreen that looked out over the water, two small ramps under the front wheels to level it, that one, she could hardly believe, was the one from her vision. She backed up to a tree trunk, an oak that grew alongside the narrow road directly opposite the front of the van, and leaned back on it if only for moral support. She gazed intently at the white van for a while, not daring to move for fear she fall.

Grace had not expected to find the van, how could she dream a vehicle she'd never laid her eyes on before? And with such precision. Déjà vu? She doubted it. Looking for pieces of the jigsaw that didn't fit, she noted the bright orange electric lead, that trailed from the side of the van and plugged into a power post. Then she made towards the two remaining motorhomes that she hadn't yet checked, just to ascertain that they bore no resemblance to the one she had found. She was satisfied, somewhat unsatisfied, maybe even frightened, that this was the one.

She took up her stance by the tree again

Should she approach the van and knock on the door? That would be really embarrassing if the owner answered and for some reason wasn't the person from the dream. And what would she say anyway, even if the owner fitted her image? Do you recognise me from a dream? 'A nutty old woman is at the door, dear, and she thinks that she dreamt of us last night!'

Better to stay and watch for a while. Partially sheltered from the wind and rain, the rain that slowly soaked through her coat, by the oak tree, that increasingly offered little protection from the elements, she shivered and waited.

There was some activity from the motorhome. Screens, like curtains, that covered the windscreen on the inside were being drawn back to let in the day. A slight creaking sound, heard from her position, signalled that someone was moving about inside and the van shifted a tad on its suspension, unrelated to the way it moved when the gusts of wind played upon its wind-break, air-brick, profile. 'Well, someone's in!' she thought.

After what seemed an age, the door opened, and a man stepped out and stood there zipping up his waterproof jacket, and she knew him. Knew him well!

Grace froze.

Chapter 14

The four gathered at the Gathering for the meal that, on Phillip's insistence, he'd pay for, and nothing would deter him from picking up the complete bill. Even the drinks were put on to his tab. Miles felt a pang of uncertainty as he estimated the final tally, a tally that he was helping to accumulate, but Phillip just took it all with a pinch of salt. When the bill arrived at the table, he didn't even flinch as he read the bottom line, he reached casually into his pocket for his wallet, removed a wad of notes from it, counted them out and added a ten percent tip, then placed the notes onto the plate along with the bill.

'Are you sure I can't help pay for this?' Miles offered once again. He'd been offering throughout the whole meal. Phillip gave him a look that could curdle milk and Miles backed off.

'There's nothing that pleases me more, than to pay for this. It's the least I can do in return for what you've done for me.' Phillip's smile never wavered. 'Besides, what else have I got to spend my money on?'

Miles didn't know what Phillip might spend his money on, but with some misgivings he allowed him to foot the cost of the expensive evening.

'How are you getting back to your hotel?' Julie asked, as the last drinks were drained.

'I'll walk, it'll do me good to get some air.'

'But it's got to be about three miles.' Julie said, knowing that the wind and rain were still fighting a battle outside.

'Not as far as I thought then!' Phillip replied. 'And I've got wet weather gear in the car, so I'll be fine. I'll wander back into the village to pick up the car in the morning.'

They stood around Phillip's car while he put on his waterproof over-trousers, helping to maintain a balance that had inexplicably escaped Phillip. 'Must be something to do with the cut on my head affecting my inner equilibrium!' Phillip said, hopping about on one leg like he'd trodden on a drawing-pin. When at last he was dressed for the journey, Phillip said goodnight and headed off at a brisk pace following the main road towards Ballachulish, while Julie and Miles walked Mhairi a short part of the way to her house, before continuing on towards the camping site.

Miles knew that Mhairi and Julie had spent quite some time discussing things privately between themselves, whilst Phillip and Miles had played a non-sober few rounds of pool. Now the wind was blowing the cobwebs away he was eager to find out whether Mhairi was fully informed on what had transpired that morning. He'd noticed Mhairi's quizzical looks in his direction after they'd finished their games and returned to the table. But he would have to wait until they got into the warmth of the van before he could ask Julie. The wind threw horizontal rain from off the loch that stung and lashed at any exposed skin, and conversation was impossible in the onslaught.

With all of their wet gear hung from any place available; the hooks in the shower cubicle, over the door and on the backs of the front seats. The fan heater set as high as it could go, and the van's own gas-fired, air-blown system humming loudly in accompaniment, Miles poured them both a nightcap and they set to the debrief.

'What did you tell Mhairi about this morning?' he asked quietly, and with a note of impending doom.

'I told her that you were having some issues, without really going into any detail.'

'How much detail did you go into?'

'I may have mentioned that you were hearing a voice in your head, and that you were pretty convinced that it was not coming from within yourself.' Miles smiled to himself and pictured how he would take similar news about someone he knew.

'So, she thinks I'm a nutter then! Did you also tell her that it might be a dragon that was talking to me?'

'I think she'd already worked that one out, I didn't really need to say anything to encourage that chain of thought.'

'So what did she say?'

Julie sat quietly for a while before she pulled a face, wrought with confusion, and answered. 'That's the funny thing, she seems to know it's a dragon, or in her words, a beithir that's talking to you. She is quite willing to believe that the beithir is real and has chosen *you* to talk to. She doesn't question it, she doesn't think it's weird at all. It's like she knows it exists and is real, but she hasn't divulged any information that tells me why she believes that.'

'What do you mean?'

'Well, I think she appears to be jealous of you. I can't explain why I think that, but I reckon she wishes it was *her* that had the voices in *her* head.'

'I wish it was her!'

'You don't mean that! She's a very strange person, she's been through so much and in anyone else, I would think that this yearning was childish, but with Mhairi-. It's not a fantasy that she's looking for, she doesn't even consider it fantastic. She seems so down to earth, but so ready to accept that this is real, almost commonplace.'

'The way she keeps looking at me is disconcerting, and when she started talking to Phillip about dragons I nearly died. Did I miss anything when I went out for a cigarette?'

'No, she took it all on herself, she steered the subject clearly away from you. Phillip didn't suspect a thing, if that's what you're worried about.'

'Well I'd rather he didn't know.' Miles thought carefully before continuing. 'Julie, do you think Mhairi has met the dragon before?'

'I don't know, I don't think so unless she's keeping it very quiet. I think she knows it's real, but I don't know if she's spoken to it.' she paused. 'Now I'm sounding like I believe in the dragon.'

'Don't you?'

'Well it's all a bit way out for me. I'm sorry, Miles, I'm just being honest, I just don't know what's happening to you, I wish I did.'

Miles considered her words and her actions to date. 'If it turns out that I'm hearing voices in my head that are mine, then you couldn't have been more understanding or supportive, you haven't judged or decried what I've been saying at all. And if it turns out it's a dragon that's been doing the talking, then I hope you will get the proof that reassures you that I'm not bonkers.' Miles grinned outwardly, but weakly and the grin was soon gone, back to the contemplative furrowed brow of before.

At a late hour, Miles turned the noisy van heating back to a tick-over setting, and they both got ready for bed. Lying under the warm duvet, he wanted to talk to the dragon again. He needed to know what the dragon planned, but he felt uncomfortable with the idea of lying there in his bed, with Julie next to him, having a quick chat with something that even Mhairi accepted more readily than he did. Within seconds he fell sound asleep.

The rain hadn't really stopped but had changed to a constant drizzle. The wind still blew hard out of the west. Miles stepped out of the van and zipped up his coat, protection from the uncaring gusts that still attempted to unhinge the motorhome from its hard standing, and the lazy rain that went through you, rather than around you. All in all the weather still carried a proportion of saltwater to be cast with hate upon the shore.

Out of the corner of his eye he saw the old lady leaning against the tree and looking in his direction, but he had more pressing concerns in the amenity block, and he cut across the grass in the direction of the toilets and showers and the relieving quality they might provide.

On his way back to the van, he followed the road that skirted the site and passed by the old lady, still attempting to shelter herself.

'Good Morning.' he greeted. She seemed to recoil at his words, to try and embed herself further into the bark she leaned back upon. Miles grew worried and stopped, and turned fully to face her. She was an elderly woman, frail, in no uncertain terms, he'd not seen her on the site before and in this weather, she must be getting cold by just standing there, she was certainly getting soaked. 'Are you alright?' he asked concernedly.

'She mustered up some fortitude and took a step towards him. Almost in a whisper she asked, 'Are you Miles?' and as the very words left her lips she seemed ready to run away from his answer. A silent battle, full of uncertainty as to the outcome, ravaged before him. Miles could discern the fear within her sunken eyes, he didn't know who she was or why she was here, but he'd heard her say his name, and he'd heard the tremor in her voice.

'Yes, I'm Miles. And you are?'

'Grace.' The way she spoke her name, it almost sounded like an apology. 'I'm Grace, and I know you!' Courage was building in her.

Miles took a step backwards in shock. It couldn't possibly be the Grace who he'd seen through the eyes of the dragon or seen with his own eyes. She was so much-older, it was like comparing two opposites. The Grace that ran towards him in tears that day, full of youth, vitality and anger; the Grace who spoke often in those ensuing days, full of woe and childish musings, and now-. This Grace who bore no resemblance at all to the one he felt he knew, aged and smaller, less significant and more unsure than her younger self.

He plucked up a little courage. 'Are you really the woman-' he felt awkward calling her a girl, 'who came to the beach after she lost her father?' Grace nodded in the affirmative.

'How did you get here?' Miles asked.

'I caught a bus!' she said with mild surprise, as if that was the answer he had meant to hear.

'I mean, how did you know to come here?'

Grace looked about her for some moral support, but with none to hand she spoke quite plainly. 'I had a vision of you and your wife, and of a dog called Skip. It showed me where to come and where you would be. I didn't believe you would be here for one minute, but I had to see for myself. And here I am. And here you are!'

Miles was left almost speechless. The dragon had proved its own existence by encouraging something, impossible for him to know, to actually happen. He looked at Grace and saw that she was trembling slightly, not sure if it was due to the cold or due to the improbability of their meeting, he remembered his manners.

'Won't you come into the warm and- perhaps a cup of tea?'

Grace searched for a reason to refuse the offer, but for some reason she felt Miles posed her no threat. She walked slowly and unsteadily towards him, he offered his arm for her to take and together, they finished the short distance to the van. Miles opened the door and called inside to let Julie know that they had a visitor. Julie got up from her seat and stood open-mouthed as

Miles helped Grace up the step and into their domain. 'This, is Grace.' he said by way of introduction, and even he couldn't believe it.

Grace took a seat in the motorhome, scanning about her to take in her new, unfamiliar surroundings. Her eyes located the cushions that were propped up at the ends of the upholstered bench seats, two of them were decorated in needlepoint with Skip's image. 'Was that your dog, Skip?' she pointed towards one of the cushions.

Julie answered. 'Yes, but how do you know his name?'

'Because I had a dream and I saw him, and both of you too.'

'But that's impossible!' Julie complained.

'That's what I would have said a few minutes ago, but it isn't impossible, because I'm here and your husband knows me, I can see it in his eyes, he knows me.'

Julie looked at Miles who remained standing by the small kitchen area in the van. 'Is this the Grace you told me about only yesterday?'

'Apparently, it is.' Miles answered and realised they were talking about her as if Grace was not even there. 'I'm sorry Grace, it's all come as a bit of a shock to the both of us. I had no idea that this might happen, I'm sure you didn't too.'

'How much do you know about me, Miles?'

'Well if what I know is all true, then I know everything you said on the beach after your father died in the war, and more, and I've only known it since yesterday morning.'

'But that's impossible, it can't be so!' she remonstrated.

'Grace, I saw you running across the beach, crying. I saw you curled up in a ball and I heard you scream for death to take you. I saw each and every visit you made to that beach until the very last!'

'So what did I talk about on my last visit?'

'You talked about how you'd be going to Glasgow that evening, how you'd miss being here, how you didn't want to go but you had to. You cried and said it was all so unfair, you suddenly fell into a foul temper and you started throwing stones and screaming. Nothing could be said that would calm you and eventually you just marched away. Was that about right?'

Grace nodded and visualised her last afternoon in the glen she loved, but the glen she couldn't remain a part of any more. She retrieved a tissue from a small plastic packet in her pocket and dabbed at her eyes with it.

Miles set to making a cup of tea, allowing Grace to wallow in her thoughts; Julie just sat, dumbstruck by what she was seeing. Once a steaming mug of tea was placed before her on the small occasional table, and a packet of biscuits were opened, Miles asked. 'What happened after you went to Glasgow, Grace?'

She mulled over how much she should say before answering. 'I went back to school, kept my head down, and had an ordinary life.' She didn't want to expand upon any of what she said. 'Look, I'm sure you are really nice people but I can't be here right this minute. Please understand, I've been dreading this moment for all the years I've been living locally, and I need to think hard about what all of this is about.' She rose to her feet, ignoring her full cup of tea, and started towards the door.

Miles couldn't stop her, nor did he want to, they all had so much more to think about now.

'How will you get back home?' Julie asked, stalling Grace's flight.

'I'll get the bus.'

'You can't just wait at the bus stop in this weather.' said Julie. 'Why don't I make a phone call to a friend and get him to drive you home, you can finish your tea in the meantime and we won't talk about anything if that's what you want, will we Miles?' She gave him a menacing look.

'Please, finish your tea.' pleaded Miles. Grace retook her seat and picked up the steaming mug. Julie dialled a number into her mobile phone and spoke when Phillip answered.

'Phillip, can you do me a huge favour, can you come to the caravan site and pick up a lady called Grace and take her home.' she looked at Grace and asked 'Where do you live?'

'Kinlochleven.' she replied softly.

Phillip was only too happy to oblige, after he got directions to the site and their whereabouts within it, he said he'd be there in ten minutes or so. Julie looked back at Grace and said 'He'll be here in a few minutes.'

'Who's Phillip?' Grace wanted to know.

Julie described their meeting of him, how he'd had a slight accident on the steps into the Gathering, and that of their subsequent meeting less than eighteen hours earlier, one that stretched out into the evening. Grace listened and took a sip of her drink. Miles cautiously offered her the packet of biscuits and she took one to dunk into her tea.

'How much does Phillip know of what's going on?' she asked.

Miles chose to reply. 'Nothing at all, he's just a really nice gentleman who's up here on holiday on his own.' And Miles wanted it to stay that way, but he'd never say that.

'He won't hear anything from my lips.' Grace said, almost tapping into Miles's mind.

'Thank you.'

'You're English, aren't you?' Grace asked after a short period of communal silence.

Miles answered uncertainly, 'Yes we are.' and wondered about the point of her line of questioning.

'I just didn't think you'd be English, I thought you'd be- Scottish, Gaelic-speaking even!' Miles couldn't begin to fathom why they shouldn't be English and decided to change the subject to the weather. They chatted away amiably, the tension between them evaporating away, until Phillip arrived and knocked on the door to the motorhome. Grace got up and Miles and Julie raised to their feet as a sign of courtesy. She moved to the door, Julie and Miles allowing her the room through the narrow confines of the van. Miles opened the door and stepped outside first, holding the door open for Grace to follow. He greeted Phillip and thanked him for taking the time to give his service. After a short introduction to Phillip, Miles escorted Grace to the passenger side of the car and she got in.

Before the door was closed, Grace spoke. 'You English always talk about the weather, I usually find that bloody annoying, the weather is what it is and there's nothing you can do about it, but I think I will see you again, Miles.' She spoke her words with an amount of confidence that surprised Miles and possibly shocked Phillip who looked at Miles with a question on his face that asked 'What have you done?'

The car left the site at a very sedate pace, as Miles thought it would. 'Grace would be safe with Phillip.' He thought as he stepped back into the van.

'Well that was strange.' said Miles as he sat down opposite Julie.

'I can't believe that actually happened. I'm not sure which of us is more surprised. Grace was actually shaking with fear, you could see it.' said Julie.

'I thought she might be cold, but when we got into the warm, she still didn't stop shaking. I think she was scared to pick up her tea incase she dropped the mug.'

'At least it sort of proves that there is a dragon. You couldn't have foreseen the arrival of Grace, it's impossible. The dragon has proved himself!'

'So what happens next?' asked Miles. Julie shrugged her shoulders in reply.

Phillip made small talk with Grace on the short, time-lengthy drive to Kinlochleven. He didn't feel the need to be concerned with what had happened that had brought Grace to the site in Invercoe, and he didn't question Grace about it either. Grace asked him about his holiday and he answered honestly, though omitting the part about his illness. Phillip was easy to talk to, he didn't have any preconceptions and he didn't jump to any instant opinions regarding anybody. He thoroughly enjoyed the chance meeting with Grace and her company for the few miles he travelled with her, and she enjoyed his company too. So much so, she almost forgot why she'd been at the site in the first place.

Phillip pulled the handbrake on, outside of Grace's home, got out of the car and rounded it, to open the door for Grace. Grace thought that if there had been a puddle on her walk to the front door, Phillip would have produced a cloak and thrown it down for her to tread upon. He escorted her to the front door, the radiant smile never leaving his face, and she in turn smiled back at him.

'Would you care for a drink?' she found herself saying, without even flinching or worrying about what the neighbours might think. 'I'm sorry, that's so un-lady-like, too presumptuous.'

'I'd be honoured.' Phillip replied. 'And *you* could never be anything other than Lady-like.'

Phillip, on accepting her kind offer, followed her into the house, he was shown into the sitting room where he took a seat.

'I can do a tea or a coffee, or maybe you would prefer something a little more Scottish?'

'I think a little bit of something Scottish would be perfect just now.' Phillip answered with a cheeky wink and a beaming grin, and suddenly Grace felt a portion of her years tumble away from her.

'So it is!' she replied.

Chapter 15

Mhairi stood in the hallway, her back against the front door, looking into to her small studio with squinted eyes. She'd spent the majority of the previous night applying layers of paint to a large canvas mounted on her easel, and in the broad light of day she still wasn't satisfied with the results. When it came to landscapes, she usually worked from a photograph of the scene she wanted to depict, sometimes she enhanced the source image by removing colours or resetting the saturation points until she was happy with the original image upon a computer. She'd do this until she was certain she was heading in the right direction and then, and only then, she'd start plastering on the acrylic paint onto the canvas. Her new painting didn't have a source, other than the one that was in her mind, and the distant canvas wore paint in a way that didn't express what she was imagining.

Walking through to the small kitchen she clicked the button on the kettle to boil, and pulled down a mug from the cupboard above. With a fresh black coffee in her hand, she returned to the studio and sat in front of the easel. 'Why is this so difficult?' She contemplated the work while blowing and sipping at the strong reviver. 'I mean, it's a dragon! But is it a beithir?' She hit the nail on the head as she talked to herself.

The canvas definitely portrayed the abstract likeness of a dragon, but it was just that. A dragon. Dragons had been done to death by hundreds of fantasy artists, any town with a gallery would have, at some time, dealt with a depiction of the infamous beast. The wings, the claws, the scales, the redness, the nostrils, the tail and the fire, all pointed at the artwork in front of her being a dragon, but the piece didn't have the depth or the uniqueness that made it a beithir. She placed her mug down and removed the canvas from the easel, turned it about so she couldn't see the painting and leaned it against the wall to join with a host of other uncompleted works.

Needing to move away from anything to do with paint, Mhairi picked up her coffee and took it with her to a seat in the kitchen. On the small table in front of her sat her laptop and she thought about research. Opening the device up, she switched it on and waited for the home screen to be displayed, then she typed in her search word 'beithir' into the browser, and she selected to see the results as images scrolling through them as they accumulated on the screen. It seemed that the beithir had taken on many shapes and forms, some had a ridiculous amount of legs, some were serpentine and others were dragon-like. Nothing stood out so she abandoned the search and typed in 'fuath' instead. More images sprang onto the screen, but none evoked the sentiment she was striving to achieve.

Just knowing the story of the beithir wasn't going to get a painting done, she needed to speak to someone who'd seen the creature and discuss it with them. Miles was that person, of that she was certain, even though she'd never been told outright that he had seen the beithir. Mhairi had amassed tiny subtle clues and had come up with a whole number. 'But what if I'm wrong? What if Miles only has a passing interest in dragons, an interest that's based purely upon curiosity?' She pondered her future actions. Julie had said that Miles was hearing a voice in his head, if she were to ask Miles about that, he would likely clam up. If she asked about dragons, maybe she could get away with it. She could broach the subject, and she could be honest with him, after all, it was his opinion she sought, it didn't really matter if he'd not seen a beithir, only his thoughts mattered, irrelevant of his state of mind.

Regardless of proof, one way or another, as to Miles's experience, or lack of, Mhairi put on warm clothing and walking boots, and left the house bound for the campsite. She elected not to phone ahead, well, what could she say on the end of a phone? She just had to wing it. She walked purposely, following the road, across the bridge and into the caravan site.

Phillip's car was parked in front of the motorhome and it caused her to halt her advance, she didn't feel it would be prudent to continue if they already had visitors. She observed from a distance as an old lady was helped into the passenger seat of his car, and then she watched as the car was driven across the site towards the exit gate and the road. Once Miles had stepped back into the van and the door was shut again, Mhairi resumed her walk towards it at a snails pace.

'Thought I'd drop by, any chance you could tell me about what a beithir looks like?' that wouldn't work. 'Is there any chance I can speak to you alone about your thoughts on dragons?' no! 'I'm having a problem with my painting and wondered if you could help!' She glimpsed at the palms of her hands as they helped stress her vocal gambit and saw that they really did indicate a problem with her painting. Dried dark, acrylic paint smears appeared like the tattoos on the backs of her hands, she wouldn't wash them off, not yet.

She reached the van and knocked gently on the door. Almost immediately Julie opened the door to her and invited her in. 'What brings you here? Come in, please.' The expression on Julie's face reassured Mhairi that she was, indeed, very welcome at that moment. Mhairi climbed the step into the vans warm interior and made to taking off her boots before treading upon the carpeted floor.

'Was that Phillip just leaving?' she asked, not wanting to appear nosey, and struggling with the limited space available to remove ones boots on a small door mat.

Julie watched her dilemma for a few seconds. 'Don't worry about the carpet, just come inside and sit down, take your boots of when you're sitting, we always do.' she said keenly. Mhairi took the vacant seat opposite Miles and continued to remove her boots, then she struggled off her coat and placed it on the back of the drivers seat.

'We've just had a rather strange meeting.' Miles announced. His eyes shone with a light that Mhairi hadn't noticed before, he seemed exceedingly happy, and for now, more alive than he had ever appeared to her before.

'With Phillip?' she asked, slightly confused.

'No, with Grace!' Mhairi still didn't know what he was getting at, though she thought she should know, given the way Miles had exclaimed it so proudly.

'Who's Grace?' she asked apologetically.

'You remember the story you told us, about the young girl in the village who spoke to Death and ran from the church?'

'Of course.'

Miles looked triumphant. 'That, was Grace!'

'The woman that just left with Phillip, that was the same person from all of those years ago?' Mhairi needed just a little more confirmation to get onto the same page as Miles and Julie.

'That was the same Grace.' said Julie.

'But how did you meet her? How did you find her?'

Miles answered. 'She came to us, she was just standing over there, by that tree, this morning, looking at the motorhome,' He pointed absently out, towards the road through the windscreen. 'I said good morning and she came over and spoke my name, and Julie's, and that of our old dog, Skip. She knew about all of us! Phillip's just taken her back home, it seems she was a little frightened with what was happening.'

'I don't blame her for being frightened. How did she know to come here and why?'

'Apparently she had a vision that we featured in.'

'But why would she have a vision about you? No offence, but you've only been here a few days, so why you?'

Miles had been sitting conspiratorially forward until Mhairi asked her question, now he sat back and leaned upon one of the cushions that portrayed the image of

Skip. He considered how much he should tell her. 'I don't know, why us!'

Mhairi did not believe his answer and looked towards Julie, sat next to her. 'You can't just tell me that small snippet of information and expect to get away with it, I know there is more you're not telling me, I can see it in your eyes Miles.'

Julie answered on Miles's behalf in explanation. 'I told you that Miles was having some issues, imagining he was being spoken to.' Miles visibly tried to sink further into the cushion, and Julie watched him carefully. 'How open-minded are you Mhairi?'

'I suppose I'm very open-minded, I try to be an artist, I suppose I like to look at things without too much judgement. I wasn't taken aback when you told me about Miles hearing voices.' She looked back at Miles's eyes, they looked less- in control, they flitted about not wanting to make direct contact with her own.

'You may as well tell her the whole story, Miles.' Julie prompted.

'What do you know so far?' Miles asked after clearing his shaky voice with a throaty cough.

'I'll tell you what I believe I know, then you can correct me if I'm wrong. How does that sound?' Mhairi spoke forcefully but compassionately. She wanted to pave the way for Miles, it couldn't be easy for him.

'Okay.'

She continued in a hushed tone. 'I think you've seen a beithir, and with what I've just heard, I think Grace saw a beithir too all those years ago.'

'Why do you think that?'

'Well, it was your interest in the dragon and other mythological beasts. Nobody I have ever met has talked about those topics, very few people outside the glen even know the story of the beithir. Your keenness to find out about dragons was way too great to be a passing interest. Who on earth talks about dragons the first time they meet someone anyway?'

'So maybe I'm just a little out of the ordinary, Poirot!'

'Miles, I like you for being a little bit out of the ordinary, but I really do believe you've seen a beithir, and, I think the voices you've been hearing are the beithir talking to you.'

'He said he was a dragon!' Miles felt stunned by the words as they left his lips.

'So you have seen a dragon?'

Miles smiled at Mhairi. 'I suppose I have.'

Julie spoke. 'Mhairi, how the hell did you come up with that conclusion based upon what you've heard?'

'I think, I wanted it to be something special. I want to believe in something that's there, something completely different from the normal.' she took a deep breath. 'Look, I've spent the majority of my life going backwards and forwards to this hospital or that, nothing special has ever happened to me unless you consider these burns as special.' She rolled up a sleeve to show her scars. 'These have been the bane of my life and are a permanent reminder, they also seem to be able to repel people faster than I can, left to my own devices. I spent most of my childhood just reading stories of all those fantastic things that happened to other people, but never to me, I want something special too, I want something incredible to happen, that's for me alone!'

A tear formed in the corner of her eye. 'I do my painting and a bit of bar work every now and then, but I feel trapped in the glen where a stream of interesting people come and go and nothing ever changes.'

'Maybe it has now.' Julie comforted.

Miles had listened intently and knew he should share everything that had happened to him, with Mhairi. He stood up and reached down three glasses from the cupboard above Mhairi, he placed them on the small table and pulled down a bottle of whisky. 'Will you?' he turned the bottle in his hands to show her the label on the bottle.

'I don't usually, sun over the yard-arm and all that, but why not!'

Miles poured three whisky's out and passed them round. Sitting forwards again and cradling his own glass in both hands, ignoring eye contact, he told them both his story. He didn't leave anything out, from the moment he met the dragon to the meeting of Grace, all in chronological order, day by day. He even tried to explain his feelings of fear, and of the acceptance that he might be going mad. He laid everything out on the line, finally sitting back to look into the awestruck faces of his audience.

'So, now you know. What do you think?'

He hadn't told Julie certain parts of what had happened, and he sat slightly fearful of what she would say as well, now he had laid himself totally bare to both of them.

Mhairi broke the short silence that pervaded the air. 'You saw Grace on every one of her visits to the beach, what was she like?'

'She was a child, a pretty little girl who was angry and upset. She assumed she was speaking to Death and she could never accept it as being anything else. Her life was ruined, she did most of that to herself,' Miles thought about his own revelation. 'much in the same way I've probably ruined my life by telling you about what happened to me.'

'You've not ruined your life.' Julie said. 'In fact, I think you've enhanced it in my eyes.' she reached across and stroked the back of one of his hands.

'That's down to being in the company of two extraordinary women.' he fawned.

Julie pulled her hand back in mock contrition.

'I came here today to ask you what the beithir, or dragon, looks like. I've been trying to paint one and have failed miserably because I keep treating it like every dragon you've ever imagined. You've made it so easy for me to ask that question now. So what does the dragon look like?' she turned her palms upwards to show Miles the paint scars as proof.

'Well it's not a dragon, I can tell you that, not in the way we consider dragons to be. To me, the voice wants to be focused on the bones of a boat-wreck upon the beach. It's totally inanimate, a structure that's man made and rotting away. The voice I hear comes from inside my head though, it just tells me that its actually the wreck that's speaking, like I have to have something to focus on. It's sort of very hard to explain, it's inside me yet my focus has been directed towards the skeletal remains on the beach.'

'The fuath are water spirits,' Mhairi stated. 'I suppose as long as there is a presence of water they could take the form of anything they wanted. If the beithir is a fuath, that might explain why it's able to appear to be the boat. What did Grace say?'

'She hasn't said anything yet.' Miles answered.

'Will she be back?'

'I hope so.'

The three of them slowly sipped at their whisky's and ruminated over the possibilities that the dragon was a beithir, that the beithir was one of the fuathan, and as to why it had chosen Miles to speak to. Nothing seemed conclusive and further speculation taught them nothing new or revealing.

'Miles?' asked Julie. 'You told us that you spoke to the dragon without actually being near it, you said it could hear everything that went on around you, you told us you even contacted the dragon from the craft shop. Can you speak to it now?'

'I don't know, I've never tried with anyone else around, being aware of what I'm trying to do.'

'Can you try for me, now?' Mhairi looked on expectantly.

'I'll give it a go. What should I say?'

'Just ask it if it has heard our conversation, and if it has, what it thinks?'

Miles concentrated his mind to ask and the answer came back before he'd even formed the words into an adequate sentence. It boomed into his head. 'Yes Miles, I can hear you all, and in answer to your speculation, maybe I am one of the fuathan. I also think I must be the beithir here, but isn't that just a label you like to put upon things, like why you call butter, butter, and not jam'

'That's non-sensical, I see what you mean though, I am a man and that's a name we men have decided upon for ourselves. Can I ask, do you mind me talking to other people about you, like this?'

'Not in the slightest, I'm finding it rather interesting, your musings.'

'Can I just hold you there for a minute?'

'I'll still be here, Miles.'

Miles looked at the two expectant faces opposite him. 'He's here.' he said, and in a way, the sound of what he said reminded him of Jack Nicholson in 'The Shining', when he stuck his head through a hole in a door and said, 'Here's Johnny'

'What did you ask the dragon?' Mhairi asked.

'I asked him about whether he minded being discussed in this way, and he doesn't. He seems to find it rather interesting, actually. He also told me he might be classed as the beithir or one of the fuathan.'

Mhairi unexpectedly and excitably cut in and blurted out. 'Can I speak to the dragon?'

'I don't know.' Miles listened to how childish his reply sounded, almost hoping he was the only one the dragon could speak to. 'I could ask.' he said in reparation. 'I'll ask if either of you could speak to the dragon, rather than through me.'

The voice spoke. 'This is quite irregular, Miles. Do you want me to try and speak directly to both Julie and Mhairi?' In Miles's mind he thought he might be relinquishing some of the control of the situation he'd striven so desperately to attain, and he wasn't so sure that he was happy with giving up some of the specialness he felt he had. 'Do you want me to try, Miles?' The voice was more commanding than before.

Miles thought of Mhairi's own admission, that her life had been so fraught with pain and emptiness and that she craved something special to happen to her. What could be more special than this? He looked at Julie's face and tried to read what was going on behind her beautiful blue-grey eyes. 'Would you both like me to ask whether he can speak to you?'

Julie considered her own thoughts, even delving into her own religious beliefs before answering. 'Not for me, love. I don't think I need that in my life at the moment. Besides, Ive got you to look after, and that's enough for me.' She smiled at him.

'Mhairi?' Miles turned his attention back to the beautiful young woman that bore those horrendous burns, but with such dignity, as Miles saw it.

'Yes!'

Mhairi's whole face lit up, every feature appeared to glow in ecstasy, then the tears streamed from her eyes, she placed the whisky glass back on the table quickly before hugging at her knees like in a gesture of prayer or pre-birth. She looked about her trying to position what was happening and locate where it was coming from, and she cried, more than she'd ever cried before, but in absolute happiness.

Julie looked upon the rapturous Mhairi and then at Miles as he stared at her, vacantly studying her, seemingly devoid now of the gift he'd once owned.

Chapter 16

Phillip phoned Julie up at about noon to confirm that Grace had been returned home safely and that they were having a wonderful time together.

'Are you still there then?' Julie asked a little surprised, 'The dirty old dog!' she thought.

'Yes I'm still here, I just thought you might like to know that we're going to the Clachaig for some lunch.' Julie imagined Phillip winking.

'But you don't even know Grace! You've only just met her.'

'Life's too short for that sort of thinking, so I've invited her for lunch and she's accepted.'

'You never cease to amaze me, Phillip. You're a sly old devil aren't you?'

'I like her, and we've found plenty to talk about since we left you.'

'Does Grace know you're talking to me?

'Yes.' He paused for a moment before continuing 'Why do you ask?'

'Is there something you're not telling me. Phillip?'

'No, I don't think so. All I'm saying is, that we are going to the *Clachaig* to get a meal and, if you happen to be there, or not, that's the way it happens!' he put a stress on the word, Clachaig, to emphasise the importance of what he was telling her.

'What does Grace think?

'It's her idea that I let you know. God knows why? That woman tells me nothing!'

Julie could faintly hear some chiding words from Grace in the background, so unbecoming a woman of that age, and began to work out a new line of questioning. 'Phillip, is Grace drunk?'

'Maybe a little tiddly, just one or two wee one's'

'What have you done?'

'Nothing.' Phillip sounded bemused.

'How much has Grace told you about why she was here?'

'That's the strange thing, she's told me absolutely nothing. I can't wait to find out what this is all about.'

'Okay Phillip, I'll tell Miles and Mhairi. By the way, I don't think Mhairi's opening the shop today, she's here with us now.'

'It'll be good to see you all, if you happen to be in the *Clachaig* for lunch.' there was that stress again then Phillip hung up and left Julie staring at the dead mobile-phone in her hand.

'Well?' asked Miles.

'It seems that Grace doesn't mind seeing us again, Phillip's taking her to the Clachaig for lunch, and it sounded like an open invitation from Grace. I think she's drunk! Phillip mentioned a couple of wee one's'

'I expect a couple of drams has settled her down a bit, she did seem rather jittery earlier.'

'Do we go and see Grace then?' Julie asked.

Miles looked to both women for a decision to be made. 'Well, I'm alright with going. It mightn't be too bad now Grace has an ally in Phillip. I expect she felt overwhelmed by it being with us two in our domain, at least at the Clachaig we'll be on neutral ground.'

'You make it sound like Yalta.' said Julie.

Miles looked confused and asked. 'Yalta?'

'Some big meeting of the powers after the second world war to divide the spoils.' replied Julie. 'Politics and peace talks.' she continued.

'What does Phillip know?' asked Mhairi quietly and surprising both Miles and Julie, having been so removed for the last half an hour.

'Welcome back, Mhairi. Apparently, Phillip doesn't know what's going on at all. How do you feel? asked Julie.

Mhairi had recovered somewhat from her visitation and, to an outsider, she seemed to be taking it remarkably well. 'If I didn't know better I'd say I was going nuts, that was- incredible.'

Julie asked. 'What did he say?'

'He! It was a she, it was a female voice, and it took over every ounce of my hearing, everything else just blotted out and I was wondering why you both couldn't hear it.'

Intrigued by Mhairi's disclosure that, while he heard a male voice, she was hearing a female, Miles asked. 'Does the voice sound like you should know who's speaking?'

'Yes it does, it's so familiar but I can't place where I've heard it before. It's all so crystal-clear, like I'm trapped in a room with the best of all sound systems. What's it like for you?'

'Much the same, I'm sure I've heard the voice before, but when I try to pin it down, nothing comes,'

Julie spoke. 'So the voices both of you have heard are different?' Mhairi looked at Miles and they both nodded. 'And you don't recognise them, even though they sound so familiar?' they nodded again. 'Could it be the voice of a parent?'

Mhairi answered. 'It's nothing like my mum's voice.'

Miles signalled his agreement. 'Nothing like my father's either. It would be good to know what Grace heard.'

'Mhairi, what did she tell you, your voice? Asked Julie again.

'She talked to me about my childhood, she could read my thoughts and, even though I had some control, she seemed to pluck images straight from within me. She saw the fire that-' Mhairi put forward both her hands, palms down, into the line of her sight and her hands shook minutely. 'it didn't hurt! I could see it like it was yesterday that it happened. She- looked after me, does that sound weird?'

'Not really, that's why I struggled with the word 'malevolent' when you mentioned the type of creature that it might be. It's a calming sensation you get when you are- under the influence, it's nice. Mhairi, you gave yourself up so more readily than I did. I fought it to start with, tried to prevent it from gaining access, it was only when I fully allowed it in that I felt at peace with it.' Miles remembered the meeting with the young Grace and his subsequent encounters with Dragon. 'What's your voice's name?'

'Beithir! Her name's Beithir.'

'Come on you two, it's nearly an hours walk to the pub from here and I think Mhairi might want to wash those hands before she gets there.' Mhairi looked at her painted hands and smiled.

'Can we make a stop off on the way?' she asked.

'You can wash them here, you know.' said Miles

'It's not that, there's something I've been asked to do.'

They set off at a brisk pace, wrapped up warm against the cold blustery wind. Miles led the way and Julie and Mhairi followed behind, arm in arm. 'It still doesn't bother you that I'm old enough to be your mother?'

'I don't see you like that, Julie. You and Miles are turning into my closest friends.'

'Do you have other friends, more your age?' she inquired.

Mhairi thought for a moment before answering. 'I seem to have a lot of acquaintances, not many I would truly call friends.'

'Why do you think that is? I don't mean to pry but-' Julie didn't finish.

'I tend to fend people off. I'm frightened they will feel sorry for me when they see my arms, I don't want them to. You and Miles have treated me like I want to be treated. How come Miles hasn't asked me about my burns, you must have told him?'

'No, I never told him anything of our chat about them. Miles isn't interested in how you got them and he isn't the sort to ask. If you were to tell him about them, then he'd be more curious and might even ask you questions, but otherwise, he won't make the first move, it's just not important to him.'

'You don't think he's avoiding the issue then?'

'To Miles, they're not an issue, and you should stop thinking that they are.'

'You're probably right,' Mhairi said thoughtfully. 'even though you just sounded ever so like my mother.'

'You haven't told us about your mum and dad, what are they like?'

'They're okay, well mum is anyway. She lets me get along making my own mistakes. I suppose if the proverbial hit the fan, she'd be there to help me out. Dad's just too overbearing, he wants to have me wrapped in cotton wool and to live back home, with them.'

'Why does he want that?'

'Guilt, I suppose.'

'Guilt?

Mhairi held out her free hand so that Julie could see the point Mhairi was trying to make. She pondered the scars beneath the tattoos and spoke quietly. 'He blames himself for not being able to prevent this, and then he blames himself for not being able to take the pain away, the operations, everything! I'm always telling him, what happened had nothing to do with his actions, it was fate, an accident, anything, but nothing works with him.'

'He must love you deeply, Mhairi.'

'He must. I just wish I could rid him of the guilt.'

'Maybe, in time.' Julie whispered.

They continued their walk but didn't stop at Mhairi's home. Three doors up, along the street, Mhairi opened the small wrought-iron gate that allowed access into a small front garden. Miles and Julie waited patiently by the gate on the pavement watching her go up to the front door, she rang the bell and waited. After a few seconds, the door was opened for her and with a turn of her head to signal she wouldn't be long, she entered the house and closed the door behind her.

Shortly, the door re-opened and a young black and white border-collie bounded the way from the house and down the short path, straining on its lead, full of expectancy of a walk to come. It pirouetted to turn about and tug at the lead with its mouth, bouncing on its hind legs and encouraging the towed behind Mhairi to hurry along. At the gate the dog sat obediently and waited for it to be opened, but as soon as it was, it resumed its energetic, pleasure-fuelled, dance, jumping up to be stroked and fussed by Miles and Julie.

'Her name's Skye.' said Mhairi 'She's a bit of a handful. Down, Skye! Sit and stay!' she spoke harshly and the dog slowly calmed enough to take notice of her words and sat; the long coated tail sweeping the floor behind her. 'Do you mind?' Mhairi proffered the loop of the lead towards Miles and he took it.

Miles crouched onto one knee before the small collie and started to fuss at its neck, Skye, in return for the attention, rolled from her sitting position ending up on her back, with her stomach exposed and her legs in the air demanding a belly-rub. Miles obliged and vigorously stroked and matted the long fur.

'Mhairi and Julie watched on. 'I'm sorry about Skip, Miles.' Mhairi said quietly. Miles looked into Skye's eyes then into Mhairi's, standing above him, and he re-discovered how much he missed having a dog.

'She's beautiful, who does she belong to?'

'She's the last of a litter of seven, the owner wants her to go to a good home.' Mhairi pointed back at the house. Behind the windows in the front room, the owner looked on. An old man stood, hand out to his side and placed on top of a larger older dog, paws up on the windowsill, to get a better look at her offspring and the folk who might take her away.

'She must be nearly a year old, how come she hasn't been taken already?'

'She got a broken leg and then Mr MacLeod wouldn't let her go, but now she's better and he hasn't found anyone who'll take on a one year old dog. No-one Mr MacLeod trusts at any rate.' Mhairi made a signal towards the man in the window and Miles watched him silently attaching a lead onto the collar of the dog next to him. Miles watched as the old man walked further back into the house and disappeared from view. The front door opened seconds later and the old man re-appeared and walked towards them with the larger collie at his side, walking strictly to heel.

Mr MacLeod was a much smaller man than he had appeared whilst framed by the window in his front room. He looked to be slightly older than Miles, with a complete mane of mental white hair that reached to his shoulders, unkempt and wayward. His hands made Miles's look small and he immediately pushed his right shovel-hand out towards Miles as he approached them. Miles stood up and took Mr MacLeod's hand in his own. Over the garden gate they shook hands; Miles doing his best to counter the firm, hand-numbing, vice-like grip. Miles felt like he should stand to attention in the presence of Mr MacLeod and when the man spoke, Miles's back straightened substantially.

'You'll be the folk looking to get a new dog then after you lost your last one?' The question sounded so direct and Miles looked at Mhairi quickly, his face a picture of uncertainty, and was about to answer but couldn't find the words.

Mhairi stepped in whilst Miles stumbled over what to say. 'Mr MacLeod, we were wondering whether we could take them both out for a walk for the afternoon, up the lane to the pub?'

Miles found his voice. 'She's well behaved.' he said, pointing at the mother. 'What's her name?'

'You'll be wanting to know about her parentage then, this one's Floss and her father is called Red dog.' The efficiency the old man spoke with caused Julie to turn away from him to hide her burgeoning smile. 'You can take 'em out for a walk and we'll talk about it when you get back, if I'm still up that is, how's that sound?' Mhairi opened the gate and took the leash from Mr MacLeod. Floss followed it and sat patiently next to her, waiting. Mr MacLeod turned and made for the house.

Mhairi called after the retreating Mr MacLeod. 'Is Fiona working today?'

'Aye, she is.'

'I'll get her to give you a ring when we're leaving.'

'That'll be fine then.' he replied without looking back, stepping through the open front door and with finality.

Walking into the forest with the two dogs, walking well, beside them, Miles asked. 'Why did you tell him that we were after a dog, Mhairi?'

'Because it's time, Miles!'

'What makes you think it's time?' Miles didn't want to sound slightly annoyed, but he was, and he intoned his annoyance.

'Beithir says it's time, it's time to embrace something new and put all of your sadness to one side for a while. She doesn't want you to forget about Skip, she knows Skip cannot be replaced and she wants you to think of him often and with love. But she also wants you *both* to be happy again. So she told me what I had to do. I felt there was something else too, but she says she can't tell me and she certainly doesn't want to tell you, yet.'

'What doesn't she want me to know?'

'That's just it, Miles, she said she couldn't let you know, yet.'

Miles contemplated Beithir's intervention into his life and how he led it. He looked down at the black and white collie, smiling at how it felt to be, once again, in the company of a faithful friend. Skye looked up at him, knowing she was being regarded. 'Come on Skye!' Miles set off at a run with Skye, smartly keeping pace at his side. 'Not bad for an old man, eh?' he huffed and asked of Skye as he ran.

Sitting on a log seat further up the glen, Skye curled up at his feet, they waited for the others to catch them up. Miles had had enough time to roll a cigarette and he was smoking it and idly rubbing Skye's ears as Mhairi, Julie and Floss emerged, following the path through the woodlands, towards his resting place. 'Took your time.' he said, inhaling deeply on the remains of the cigarette.

'Did you enjoy that?' asked Julie.

Miles looked at Mhairi who was sheepishly lagging behind. 'I'm sorry, Mhairi, I didn't mean to have a go. I just thought you were pushing me into doing something without asking me first.'

Julie asked. 'What do you think now?'

'I think that, if it's okay with Mr MacLeod, we have a new dog to look after.' He stood up and Julie walked to him to give him a tight hug. The lead, hanging limply from his wrist, didn't disturb the recumbent Skye.

'I knew you'd come round.'

Miles looked over her shoulder at Mhairi standing slightly aloof. 'Come here, you!' he released one arm from Julie and brought Mhairi into their embrace. After a few seconds he pulled away. 'Onwards and upwards!' he barked.

It was damned obvious that the two dogs had been this way before, as the footpath petered out at the top, just before the Clachaig, and joined with the old road, the dogs forged ahead. Crossed the road skirting the puddles, towing their handlers through the carpark and directly towards the Boots bar entrance at the rear of the inn. Miles had only seconds to locate Phillip's car, parked like an abandoned vehicle, at the front of the inn before being dragged away. At the double-door entry, the dogs stopped and waited for the doors to be opened for them. 'We have to let them off here.' said Mhairi, stooping to unclip Floss's lead from her collar. Miles released Skye and the two dogs shot into the pub and out of view to the bar entrance where they sat eagerly awaiting- something. Following the dogs into the pub and towards the bar, they saw what they were waiting for. A young girl almost sprinted out from behind the bar to give them both a treat and a welcome.

'Who you with today then, girls?' Using both hands to stroke and pat them she looked up from the two collies. 'Hi Mhairi.'

'Fiona.' replied Mhairi and walked up to her to give her a small hug.

'Are these two reprobates with you today instead of my old man?' She continued fussing at the dogs as she spoke, asking them to give her a paw in return for another treat.

'We're with some friends.' Mhairi indicated towards Julie and Miles who were stood by the bar and looking on. 'Miles and Julie lost their last dog last year and want another collie.'

'They'd better be good people then!' She sounded as direct as her father, Mr MacLeod. Loud enough to be heard by everyone that needed to hear.

'They are, Fiona. They're the best people I know.' and her voice sounded so full of pride.

'I'll be the judge of that!' proclaimed Fiona, and she still sounded just as curt as her father.

Fiona stood away from the two dogs and moved towards Miles and Julie, weighing them up as she walked. Julie recognised her from a previous visit a year ago. 'I'm Julie.' she said extending her hand.

'I'm Fiona,' she paused. 'do I know you?' she asked, trying intently to remember where she had seen her before.

'I think you'd remember our old dog, Skip, more.'

'Why's that?'

'Because last year, about this time, you were feeding him treats from behind the bar, in much the same way as you are today.'

Fiona worked through her memories, a lot of dogs had been fussed by her in the last year, but an image was slowly forming. 'Was Skip a big dog?' she asked.

'Huge in comparison to these two, with white socks and a long coat. He spent most of his time here trailing after you and he kept following you behind the bar.'

'I remember now. He used to just sit and stare at the Kilner jar with the treats in it. He knew exactly where they were kept.'

'We lost him shortly after that visit. We hung onto his ashes until just the other day when we scattered them into the river just up the road.' Julie fought back a tear.

'I'm sorry, he was a gorgeous dog, you must miss him.' Julie nodded.

Miles walked away from the bar reaching into a pocket for his tobacco tin, to escape back into his own thoughts for a few moments outside. Neither Grace nor Phillip were in the bar as he looked about for them on his way out. He walked around the building to the more recently built frontage and looked through the windows and into the restaurant beyond, but couldn't see them there either.

Back inside the bar, Julie and Mhairi had ordered drinks, placing them on a tab, and had taken seats in a small side room off from the main concourse. From where they sat they could see through into the main bar and spot anyone, in particular Grace and Phillip, if they approached the bar. Miles came back inside after finishing his cigarette and located them, he took to the bench seat opposite the two women. The two dogs left Fiona and followed him in from the bar and lay at the foot of the large table they were sat at, curled up, nose to nose, and closed their eyes.

'I can't find them.' said Miles.

'Maybe they've gone for a bit of a walk.' said Mhairi, appraising the reasons why they might not be here.

'What's there to see that you can't see from the carpark?' Miles asked, thinking only about the sublime views of the mountains.

'They could have gone to Signal Rock,' answered Mhairi. 'it's only a short walk from here.'

Miles looked down at the sleeping form of Skye and noted how very different from Skip she was. She wore the white socks that Skip had and the white of a dipped, paint-brush, tail, but she was more white than Skip overall. The flash on her forehead very nearly extended through into her long, white, collar fur, Skip had been a lot more black than white. Skye's muzzle was adorned by naughty-spots too, smudges of faint black buried under the white short fur of her snout, Miles had no idea why they were called naughty-spots, but he knew that Skip never had any. She was very pretty, just lying there, regaining the energy for another work-out.

About ten minutes after Miles's entry into the bar, the doors opened and Grace and Phillip walked in. Miles got up to meet them at the bar and took their order whilst Phillip helped Grace from her coat. Grace still seemed a bit stand-offish, but at least she was smiling now. When the drinks were passed across the counter Miles led them both into the little side room and Phillip took Grace's arm to guide her passed the pool table to join them.

After a brief introduction to Mhairi, who looked on stunned, like she was in the presence of royalty, the three women scrunched up onto the bench on one side of the table and Phillip joined Miles on the other side.

'I don't know what's going on here, but I've been told that there are rules, otherwise Grace will just turn about and leave.' said Phillip commandingly, taking on the role of the arbiter. Grace smiled appreciatively at him.

'That's okay, what are they?' Miles asked.

'Well you and I are not welcome at the moment,' Miles looked at Phillip, feeling shunned. 'after these drinks we are to leave Grace and Julie to it.' He looked at Mhairi and then at Grace. Grace gave a minute nod of her head. 'It's just thee and me that's got to leave, lad.'

'What are we meant to do?'

'Ever done any hill walking?'

'Yes.'

'Well if you feel you've got enough kit for it we could pop up the Pap of Glencoe while they all have a chat, and even if we get turned back by the weather, it'll be a fine walk.'

Miles looked at Julie expecting some input from her, maybe a rescue, but she merely shrugged her shoulders in acceptance of the way it would be. He wondered whether she would ask the right questions, the ones he had been working out in his head since his meeting with Grace that morning. It would be good that Mhairi would be there, he thought, she had enough unanswered questions of her own now. Miles knocked back his whisky and started to put on his coat, Phillip followed suit and they both left the inn for the mountains.

They stopped at Phillip's car where Phillip pulled a rucksack out from the back of the car, he slipped his arms into the straps and clipped the waist belt together before tightening it, jiggling his upper torso to find the optimum position for the bags contents and the most comfortable position for the sack itself. 'Just a rope and a few other essentials.' he said, as he closed the rear doors of the car.

Out on the road, they followed it for a few yards before picking up a rising path that led across the scrub, gaining height towards the Pap. 'What's going on between you and Grace?' Phillip asked, as they walked at a pace that Miles found rather too fast. Miles didn't know what to say, he couldn't spill the whole story out to Phillip, of that he was certain, but he had to say something.

'Nothing much.'

'Well look, if you don't want to tell me, just tell me to mind my own bloody business, but Grace was shaking with fear this morning, and I just want to know why?'

Miles developed, in his mind, a line he could tell Phillip without saying too much 'Grace was witness to something years ago, during the war, and that something she saw, I have seen too. She knows I have seen it, and she turned up on the site this morning to confront me about it.'

'So what have you both seen? Taking into account the fact that you weren't even born in the war, and that you come from opposite ends of the country.'

'I'd rather not say at the moment. I can't tell you, I'm sorry.'

'Can you answer me this? Is Grace in any danger?'

'No, I'm sure she's not.'

'What about you?'

'If you'd have asked me that a couple of days ago, I'd have said maybe, but now I don't think I am.

'Is that because of Grace?'

'I don't think so, it's to do with her and me, and now with Mhairi, but it's all under control.' Miles considered the word he'd used 'control', yes, all three of them were under control, under the control of the one thing he daredn't tell Phillip about.

'As long as you're all alright, I'll leave it at that for now!'

'Honestly Phillip, I'd tell you if I thought it would help. Maybe Grace will tell you when she's ready.'

'I hope so, Miles. She's an interesting lady and I like her. Even though I only met her this morning, I think the feeling is mutual.'

Miles needed to change the subject matter before Phillip had a chance to ask anything else that might be difficult to answer. 'How long will this route up the Pap take us?'

Phillip looked at his watch. 'At this rate, a return in under three hours.' And Miles knew he'd sleep well that night. Uncomfortably, but well.

Chapter 17

'Why did Miles and Phillip have to leave?' asked Mhairi.

'Miles didn't, but I couldn't envisage a better way of getting rid of Phillip for a while. I don't want him to know.' answered Grace. 'He'll look at things- differently if he knows.'

'Do you not want him around then?'

'The exact opposite, I want him around, I have really enjoyed his company today, but if he got to know what we were going to talk about I'm not sure he'd stay around. I've been in a similar situation before where I scared all of my friends away. He'd be like a rat from a sinking ship.' Grace looked towards a distant invisible point, troubled for a moment by the loss of her friends.

Julie took a sip from her gin and tonic. 'They're going to be gone for quite some time, aren't they?' she asked.

'I don't think they will be,' answered Grace. 'Phillip's hell bent on getting back here as quickly as possible, he said as much when we went down to Signal Rock and I told him what I expected of him.' She smiled at Julie. 'I'm afraid Miles is in for a rough ride, my girl!' Julie smiled back, imagining Miles being dragged over hill and moor and turning up too knackered to even get back to the motorhome.

'What did you tell Phillip?' Mhairi asked.

'It's easy with men, you tell them they are the important ones and they always do what they're told, all I said to him was that I didn't want Miles around, he asked how long for and then he suggested the rest.' The grin on Grace's face almost matched that of Phillip's.

'What made you want to come and meet with us, so soon after you couldn't get away from us quick enough?' asked Julie.

'I had some time to think, but mainly, I have so many questions I need answering.'

'We were glad you did, because we have loads of questions too.'

'Mhairi, I know you're a local girl, your accent gives you away, but why are you here?'

'I've spoken to the beithir.'

'The beithir! What's that?'

'We think it's the same creature you spoke to.'

"Has Miles spoken to it?"

'He has, but for him it's a dragon. What was it for you, Grace?'

'It wasn't a dragon or a beithir, it was a man.' She spoke in a hushed voice and didn't feel the need to elaborate, she looked about suspiciously aware that someone might be listening.

Julie looked around the bar trying to seek out what Grace was looking for. 'No-one's taking any interest in what we're talking about, Grace. I think we can speak freely here.' she said. 'I don't know about you two but I'm feeling hungry. Poor old Miles is going to be ravenous when he gets down off of that mountain.'

'He's okay, he's got ham and mustard sandwiches. I made them before we left, when I knew what I wanted to do about Phillip.'

'You're as sly as he is.' Mhairi exclaimed and laughed.

'Comes with age, my dear.'

Julie got up and went to the bar to fetch a menu, they each selected from it. Returning to the bar, Julie placed the order and the cost was placed onto their tab. She returned to the table with a numbered ticket.

'Mhairi was just telling me that Miles only started hearing his voice on Monday, is that true?'

'Yes it is.'

'How long have you been up here then?'

'We only arrived on the Sunday evening, we came up here for lunch on the Monday and Miles disappeared in the afternoon after we got back to the motorhome. That's when it all started for him.' She didn't want to elaborate on Miles's condition the day he ran off to the beach. 'Do you still talk to your voice?' she asked, avoiding any further questioning for a while.

'It's tried talking to me but I can't seem to talk to it anymore, if I had I would have told it to go away. I think it's been giving me vivid dreams ever since, and then I had a vision of you and Miles and that's what made me come to the caravan site this morning.'

Mhairi asked. 'Why do you want it to leave you alone?'

'Because of what happened all of those years ago, we had to leave the glen and our home, it caused me nothing but trouble.'

'Miles, told us that his dragon entered his mind and laid out everything that happened to you. He said that you wouldn't listen properly to what you were being told, that you were a young girl, and, maybe, went off misunderstanding what had happened to you.' said Mhairi.

'That could be true, I suppose. I was just a wee lass then and I thought I knew everything.'

'How do you see it- what happened to you?' asked Julie.

Grace took a minute to rewind back the years before answering. 'I was angry, petulant I think. My father had just been killed in France, and I was incensed by the reverend and his words, he didn't help. I prayed to die, to be with my father again and then the man came and stopped me from wanting to die. I suppose he helped me at that moment, but I was still young and angry and I reckon I told- the wrong people. I should have kept it all to myself, then none of what happened afterwards would have occurred.' Both Mhairi and Julie looked on silently as she continued to tell them about her life after leaving the glen, about her husband and her lost child. Their food arrived and provided a welcome break from the sadness that Grace poured from her heart.

Both dogs appeared at the end of the table, noses sniffing and raised high in the air, ready to accept any morsel that may come their way. Julie reached towards them and ruffled their coats between mouthfuls, the two dogs never took their eyes off the food. If a piece of fork-skewered chicken stayed airborne for too long, between plate and mouth, Skye's paw would raise in expectancy, almost demanding a treat for the action. Julie surrendered to the two sets of pleading, brown eyes on more than one occasion. How could she not?

Once their meals were finished and they sat back, sated, Grace asked Mhairi about her experience and she did her best to explain it. Julie felt a little left out and when asked about her experiences she felt loathed to say that she had none, but she did. Mhairi spoke on her behalf and said that Julie had been given a choice to hear the voice, or not, and that she'd declined the invitation.

'Why did you do that?'

'I have my beliefs and I don't feel the need to-perhaps have them questioned.' she answered honestly. 'And besides, Miles needs someone to look after him, and I'm that person.' She looked at the two faces, both intent on her own, and felt her cheeks flush. 'Hark at us! We're sitting here like we've just attended a funeral, can we liven this up for a moment or two?' she laughed nervously.

'Mhairi stood up and said. 'I'll get some more drinks in.'

'Just put it on the tab, Mhairi.' Julie encouraged.

The afternoon went convivially along, Mhairi spoke of her art, Julie about home life back in Suffolk, and Grace about returning to the area all these years later and the changes that had happened within the area in that time. At a certain point she took them all outside and explained what the inn used to look like in her day. It was hard to visualise how very much smaller it had been back in those days.

Just over three hours from the moment they left, Phillip and Miles re-entered the bar. Miles aimed straight for the bar and ordered a pint of rarely ordered cider, which he drained before he moved away and towards their table. He eventually came towards them carrying a pint of heavy for Phillip and a large measure of whisky for himself. The two dogs roused and sought the attention of the newcomers for a while before resettling.

'Phillip spoke in a hushed tone aiming his question towards Grace 'Is everything alright?'

'Yes everything is good, come and sit down, we've all had a lovely afternoon while *you've* been gone.' Mhairi smiled at her audacity to aim her reply more at Phillip, but Phillip didn't perceive the inflection in her words, or he chose to ignore it.

'Did you get to the top?' asked Julie.

'Yes we did, he dragged my sorry arse all the way up.' Miles answered.

'What was the view like?' she continued.

'There wasn't a view, it was blowing a hoolie and covered in cloud for the last two hundred feet. Thanks for the sandwiches though.' Miles raised his hand limply and with feigned effort towards Grace in appreciation. 'Without them I'd have never got up, let alone come back. Is Phillip related to a mountain hare by any chance?'

'I don't know,' she replied. 'I only met him a few hours ago. I've been doing my best to get rid of him ever since.' Mhairi coughed lager back into her glass and proceeded to carry on coughing with Julie slapping at her back. Both in kinks, a word that Grace would have to later explain to Julie but only after joining in with the merriment.

Outside it grew dark and the afternoon wore to a close. Inside, the inn started to fill. Miles hadn't realised just how many holidaymakers were here, he'd barely seen anybody out and about, but the Clachaig was certainly the place to be on a Friday evening. The conversations petered to a natural end. Grace looked about her with dismay as the bar filled. She'd spent too long in hiding and the crowd that was forming was not to her liking. She stood and asked of Phillip. 'If you'd be so kind as to fetch my coat, it's time we left the youngsters to it.' Phillip picked up her coat from the back of a nearby chair and held it gallantly for her to slip her arms into the sleeves. Miles stood up too, but without a job to perform.

'I shan't be a moment.' Phillip said, as she started to do up the buttons, he walked into the busy bar and towards the toilets.

Miles looked at the diminutive Grace, she didn't seem as frail as she had that morning, her cheeks had taken on a rosy glow and the dark rings around her eyes were lessened. Even her eyes seemed to contain a glint of sunshine that hadn't been there before. 'Thank you for coming, Grace.' he held forward his hand to take Grace's and held it lightly and politely.

'Will you be in in the morning?' she asked, as soon as she saw that Phillip was far enough away as to not overhear.

'Yes, we will be.'

'I'll pop by then, if thats okay with you two?'

'That's fine by us.' said Miles looking over at Julie for affirmation.

After Phillip returned they both headed through the main bar and towards the door, Grace gave a friendly little wave in their direction and Phillip opened and held the door for Grace to make her exit.

'We're going to have to get these dogs back soon,' Miles said, as he re-took his seat. 'and it looks like I might have to pay the bill before we go. He reached into a pocket to retrieve his wallet.

'Give me your card, Miles, I'll go up and pay while you finish your drink.' Julie got up and walked to the bar carrying Miles's wallet.

'Mhairi, How did your beithir know that Skye was looking for a home?'

'I let her in, she wanted to know about me, and I just allowed her to traipse through my mind. It felt like it was for hours that she wandered everywhere, but I know it was all over in a flash. Certain images seemed to be lingered over, like when I got these burns and I didn't have to explain them, she sort of knew. Another was of me walking these two, I often take them out,' she pointed at Floss and Skye. 'and it was one of the things that came into my head. Beithir seemed to allow me more time on the dogs, she wanted to know all about them and I pictured all about Skye, before we moved onto other things that have happened. Afterwards, she told me what she wanted me to do and I didn't see any reason not to. Have I done something wrong?' She looked at Miles apprehensively.

'No. I've just spent the last few hours going through this and that, running after Phillip, and I just couldn't work out how this all came to be.' He reached down to Skye and stroked the dog gently behind her ears.

'Do you want to keep Skye?'

Miles answered after a few seconds. 'I think I have to! Not to say I'm being forced to, but I really think it's meant to be. Skye and me. Skye, Julie and me.' He corrected, Miles added a short hummed snort, as if all the pieces of the jigsaw were in the right place and he was satisfied with the result.

Julie walked back to them smiling, making a circuitous route and dodging patrons wielding pints of beer. 'That bloody Phillip!'

'What's wrong, love?'

'He's already payed the bill!'

'So?'

'He only had two drinks, and he's payed for three meals and all of the other drinks too.'

'Seems our Phillip is a very generous man.' said Mhairi. 'I wonder where he gets all his money from?'

'Oh, Phillip's done alright for himself over the years,' said Miles. 'for one thing, he never got married, never had that constant drain on his wallet. That, and he had a well payed job!'

Julie reached out to hit at Miles but he dodged away. 'What did he do?' she asked.

'He was an accountant, and had his own accountancy firm.'

'He doesn't look like an accountant.'

'What should an accountant look like then, Julie?'

'I don't know.' she visualised her idea. 'Cardigans and suits, that sort of thing, warm comfy slippers in the evening.'

Miles glanced at Mhairi smirking in the corner. 'What should female artists look like then?' she asked.

'Well, I see them with long flowing hair, quite unkempt, T-shirt, dungarees covered in paint and sandals.'

'You're very perceptive, Julie!' The short haired, walking-booted, blouse and trouser clad, Mhairi said, and laughed.

They dropped the dogs off at Mr MacLeod's and after talking to him, it was decided that Miles was indeed a fellow who needed a dog in his life. Fiona had said as much on the phone to her dad when they'd set off on the walk back. On the topic of money, Mr MacLeod couldn't be budged, he explained that the dog's broken leg had cost him dear, money he'd never recover, and how could he put a price on that, she was priceless? Miles had started to worry about whether he'd be needing a loan from Phillip, when Mr MacLeod burst out laughing. The sum of nothing was agreed, so long as they brought her back for a visit before they left for home. They could pick her, and her favourite toys, up tomorrow.

'I'd rather see her go to a good home for nothing, than a bad one for a million pounds. And our Fiona remembers your old dog so well, she was so sad to find out you lost him, I wish I had seen him.'

'Thank you.' stammered Miles.

'Well, until tomorrow then.' Mr Macleod said brusquely, and turned and led Floss and Skye into the house.

Miles smiled to himself, people were so hard to read sometimes, he thought. 'We need to get a few bits for Skye now, bowls and such!'

Julie gripped his arm. 'Skip's are still under the seat in the van, won't they do? I think there's some toys there too.'

Three doors down, Mhairi invited them in for a coffee. They accepted the invitation and followed her into the house. She showed them around the small studio and then guided them into the sitting room at the front of the house.

With coffees in place, Miles found out what he'd missed, while in the company of the madman on the mountain. And Julie and Mhairi found out, the little that Miles was willing to share, about the accountant.

Chapter 18

Miles woke early, partly because of the envisioned excitement of being with Skye, partly because he'd spent an uncomfortable night with his muscles and limbs trying to re-create what they'd done the previous day. They just didn't want to give in to the regime of sleep and kept twitching, as if the walk wasn't over yet. They didn't hurt, they just wouldn't stop. Eventually, Miles gave up on sleep for the most part, to try and figure out why the dragon wanted Skye to have a home with him. He was in no doubt, certain, that Skye was a gift from the dragon, but he couldn't reason why the dragon felt he deserved such a gift. Thoughts on the matter, and other burning questions too, drifted in like confetti on a breeze, soon to be scattered. Some pieces would be irretrievable, others, just bounced backwards and forwards in his mind, to be ignored, forgotten or further examined. Nothing gelled, or yelled out to him, that he had any answers. The night was long.

Grace would be along around half past nine, he surmised, trying to piece together the bus timetable in his head, something he knew he could deal with, and he wanted to be back at the motorhome with Skye in tow, before she got there.

At eight o'clock he left for Mr MacLeod's, leaving behind Julie, just in case Grace's arrival was earlier than expected. As he walked, he thought through a myriad of new questions he wanted to ask of Grace and he soon saw the biggest of the stumbling blocks, firmly fixed in place. With everything he wanted to understand, through the medium of speech alone, it could take days to achieve, not the hour or so that he thought Grace might stay around for. He contemplated whether the dragon might help, but he wasn't sure if Grace would allow that to happen.

A second problem came into mind. Tomorrow, he and Julie were meant to be leaving for Fort Augustus. He couldn't see that happening now, not with so many loose ends to tie up. And, they'd only just started to know Mhairi and Phillip, they couldn't just leave, not like that.

Miles arrived at Mhairi's home, knocked on the door and Mhairi answered it, dressed and ready to venture out. At Mr MacLeod's house, Skye bounded around at their feet as they walked up the path towards the already open door to the house. Mr MacLeod was well prepared for their arrival and after only a few minutes, Miles walked back towards the campsite with a lead in his hand and Skye attached to the other end. Skye eager to walk at heel and casting quick glances at Miles's face as he encouraged and praised her.

Mhairi drew the short straw and carried two heavy carrier bags, crammed with food, bowls and toys, but she didn't mind the burden. She smiled, watching Skye's behaviour and that of Miles as Mhairi followed behind them. In her eyes, Miles was like a child with a shiny new toy.

'We were meant to be moving on, tomorrow!' Miles said with a tinge of sadness, not even glancing back at Mhairi.

Mhairi quickly caught up with Miles, span him about and looked up into his eyes. They both stopped walking for a moment. 'Will you be going?' To Miles, she sounded disappointed and spoke with urgency.

'I haven't spoken to Julie yet, but I don't want to go. There's still too much unanswered.'

'Can't you stay for a few more days?' she asked hopefully.

'I can't see a reason why not, but I need to speak to Julie first.'

'Let me speak to her, Miles.'

Miles felt slightly strange, somewhat detached, as he pondered on their meeting with Grace, he wasn't sure how well it would go, but at least it had been Grace's suggestion that she meet up with them again. 'Time would tell.' he thought to himself.

They continued the walk back in silence. Skye fell into pace with Miles and Mhairi followed, wondering what she could say that would prevent them from leaving. At the motorhome, Julie watched as they approached and opened the door for them, timing it to perfection for their arrival. Inside, Skye was the new centre of attention, she was fussed, she explored, she was played with and eventually she found her corner and curled up on a rug placed there for her to sleep.

Grace arrived at a quarter to ten, and once sat with a cup of tea in her hand, she dived right in to her reason for being there. 'Miles, I want to know what you see when you speak to your dragon?'

It was truly direct. Miles had thought he'd be the inquisitor and hadn't considered that Grace had questions of her own to ask. 'What I see is the skeletal remains of a boat upon the beach, it's been there for years and is just rotting slowly away.'

'You said that you saw me when I was a child, was the boat there too?'

Miles brought the images back into focus. 'Yes, it was there then, just with a bit more paint and a little more- complete.'

'Where is it, exactly?'

Miles described the portion of beach and the path leading down to it, through the scrubland and the rocks. Grace listened thoughtfully before looking across at Mhairi. 'Do you know where he means?'

'Mhairi spoke with a certain amount of caution. 'I know the spot Miles is talking about, but there's something wrong with his description.'

'That's what I'm thinking too.' said Grace.

'What's wrong with it?' asked Miles.

Grace ignored his question and turned to face Julie. 'Do you know where he means?' she asked quietly.

'I think I know where he means, but-'

Miles cut her off. 'What is wrong with the place? Miles almost screamed.

Grace answered him. 'There isn't a boat there, there never has been. It wasn't there when I was a child and it isn't there now! Once a week I sit on a bus and pass the area you've told us about, I look out over the loch, and the boat just isn't there.'

'Of course it's there!'

'It isn't, Miles.' Mhairi said gently, and Julie nodded her head in agreement.

'When we went for that walk and you stopped to have a cigarette, where we stopped is the place you described. I went off to give you some time smoking and I beach-combed for a while. There wasn't a boat or even the wreck of a boat there, it's all just rocks, slate and seaweed.'

Miles sat stunned for a moment, he knew that all three pairs of eyes were on him as he considered the implications of there never having been a boat there. Where did that leave him if the dragon wasn't in the form of a boat? Who was speaking to him? And where was the voice coming from? He thought quickly of something to say to avert their gaze. 'What did you see, Mhairi, when your beithir spoke to you?'

'I didn't see anything. It spoke to me and I was told it was the beithir, but it didn't have any form, it was just a voice.'

'Have you any idea what a beithir looks like?'

'No, none. I wanted to find out what it looked like but it really didn't matter in the end, it seemed to be like a spirit thing, an essence that is not bound by form.' she paused. 'What did you see, Grace? You said it was a man but what did it sound like?'

'It was a man but it didn't speak with the voice of a man, he didn't even move his lips, it spoke with a voice, I felt, I should recognise, the voice was that of a young girl.'

'Well, at least that part is the same for all of us.' said Miles, relieved to have pushed the focus away from himself. 'I hear a man's voice and Mhairi hears a woman's voice. So what can we deduce by that?'

'I think you might be hearing your own voices,' Julie stated. 'You're used to hearing them through your own ears, but you've all said that it comes from inside of you. It's got to be a more perceived sound if it can come from the inside!'

'That might be right, but Grace saw a man speaking with a girls voice.' said Miles

'The man was there, Miles, but the voice I heard didn't come from his lips. He was always there for me, but I always heard the girls voice in my head, the man just stood there, his lips never moved, he just watched me.'

'Who was the man then?' asked Julie.

'At first I thought it was Death, in fact I spent a long time believing it was he, but as time went by I knew I was wrong. Now though, I know who the man is!'

'Is!' said Mhairi.

'Who is it?' asked Miles.

She turned to look at Miles and pointed at him. 'It's you!'

'It can't be me, I wasn't even born then!'

'It was you, Miles, it was always you.'

'How do you know it was me?'

'I knew it the very first time I saw you, yesterday. You were putting on your coat and pulling your hood up, when you came back and saw me, you were wearing a wet coat, and you *are* the person I saw on the beach, wearing exactly that same coat and looking exactly like you do now. The man I saw always had a wet coat on, it glistened, he had trousers on that glistened too. At first I thought the glistening was because he was death or a spectral being, but when I saw you I knew for certain. It was because you were wearing a wet coat, the droplets of rain were beaded up on your clothing.'

'But it wasn't raining when you were on the beach!' reasoned Miles.

'It was summer, and it didn't rain for weeks,' Grace recalled. 'No-one had a coat or waterproof trousers like yours at that time. Those materials hadn't even been invented then.' Miles pictured the children he'd seen, playing in the school yard and dressed in their multi-coloured, modern, membrane fabrics; the way they glistened with the beaded water upon them. 'I saw you, Miles, wearing black, wet, waterproofs, just standing and watching me, in nineteen forty-four!'

'So you're saying my dragon can travel through time too?'

'No. I'm not saying that at all, but I think you have!' Grace was adamant. Miles struggled to believe that on the one hand there wasn't a dragon in the shape of a boat, and secondly, that his experience upon the beach was not merely a vision, but a reality.

In Miles's mind he called upon the dragon to help him understand. No crystal-clear voice came back to him. He tried again. 'Dragon?' and nothing happened. He felt trapped, like a rabbit in the headlights of a car, and he looked around furtively.

Julie noticed his afeared look. 'What's wrong, love?'

He took in all of their concentrated faces before whispering. 'I can't get the dragon to speak to me.'

'That's good, isn't it?'

Miles could not believe it was good, yet he couldn't see how it could be bad either. 'But if the dragon isn't there anymore, what does that mean? Mhairi, can you speak to the beithir?'

'I don't know!'

ESSENCE OF A DRAGON

'Try, for me.'

Mhairi closed her eyes and called out 'Beithir?' in her mind while the others looked on. After a few moments she opened her eyes again and saw their expectant faces. 'There's nothing there!' she said, saddened by the loss of something she'd so recently acquired. Grace reached a hand forward to take one of Mhairi's in a comforting gesture. They sat in silence for a few minutes.

Grace broke the silence. 'Why do you think it is, that we three, have heard these voices? What do *we* have in common?'

They looked at each other, trying to weigh up an answer. 'I heard them when I was in a foul mood after scattering Skip's ashes.'

'Mine was after I heard the news about my father.'

'Mine was because I just wanted to. I was given a choice.'

'Could it be, that we've all gone through pain, pain of loss and the pain of frustration? The beithir wanted to know about Skye,' said Miles. 'he also wanted to know about when you were a child and fell into the bonfire and got burnt. So maybe she spoke to you because-'

Mhairi interrupted Miles quickly 'I told you that about Skye, but I didn't tell you about the bonfire. How do you know about that?'

'Julie must have mentioned it.'

Mhairi looked at Julie questioningly. 'Have you said anything to Miles about how I got these burns?'

'No, and Miles has never asked.' Julie looked at Miles, concerned, his face had turned an ashen grey.

'Miles, what do you know about my burns?'

Miles pictured what he remembered before answering. 'You went to Inverness to your aunts house to celebrate Samhain, and you fell over and your arms went into the fire.'

'What else do you know about that day?'

'You were in a car, travelling up with your parents and your brother, he was being a nuisance and taunting you and got a slap across the legs for doing so, in the boot of the car there was a little red scooter and-'

'Do you know any of this, Julie?' Mhairi asked

Julie shook her head in denial. 'You told me about falling into the fire but you didn't tell me anything else about the day. You told me it was for halloween! What's Samhain?'

'I didn't think I did! Miles, where has all this come from?' she asked with urgency and ignoring Julie's question.

Miles could picture Mhairi's whole day, the day she got burnt. It seemed to him so vivid in his own memories, like it had been him that had travelled to Inverness and he that had fallen into the fire. He found he could remember the operations that followed, the journeys to and from hospitals. He saw her years at art college, her early forays into painting and he knew where her ideas came from for her works. There was no way he should know any of it, but he did with a lucid certainty. As he delved further, he saw Skye as a puppy through Mhairi's eyes, with a cast on one broken leg, looking forlorn, trapped within a dog cage, but still yearning to play.

'I don't know where it's come from, I just know it.' Miles worried at the thought that *he* had commandeered so much personal information about

Mhairi, information he felt he wasn't entitled to know. 'I'm sorry, Mhairi. I don't know how I found out any of this, but I do! I'm really sorry.' Miles wanted to cry as he tried to remove the images he couldn't stop seeing, images that belonged to Mhairi alone.

'What do you know about me?' Grace asked, breaking Miles free from the stolen memories for a while. Miles studied her time-worn face for a moment, remembering her life before her father had been killed. He pictured her mother and father and found he could describe them like they had been his own.

With resignation he said. 'I know everything about you, Grace, up until the moment when you left for Glasgow. And now I seem to know more!'

Julie looked on at Miles, and something, she couldn't put a finger on, caused her to worry for him.

Miles ran. All eyes were on him and they had bore into his skull like daggers. He ran from the van and headed towards the beach and sanctuary. His mind could no longer handle the questions he wanted to ask, in fact, it couldn't handle the questions that were certainly to come, now, from his so-called friends. The children in the playground watched his passing, a whirling dervish, screaming and screeching, flying towards an unknown destiny. A man fleeing and wearing a T shirt and socks, no boots, no coat; and then he was gone. In seconds, they resumed their games and Miles was forgotten to them

Carelessly Miles raced through the scrubland at the head of the beach and threaded the boulders that protected that same scrub from the assaults of wind and tide. He bounced off one of the last larger rocks and sprawled headlong onto the ravaged foreshore. No pain from where he'd ricocheted of the boulder, but that immovable object now gripped onto a portion of cloth, skin and blood from his left shin as Miles had taken to the air in passing it.

Miles pushed himself up from the ground and looked out upon the beach. Something inside told him the boat would be there, but he couldn't see it yet. He got to his feet and walked the final few yards, and there it wasn't. The seat, that raised mound he'd sat upon, was there, but the thing, the boat, the skeleton, the rotting hulk... wasn't. The tide was coming in, maybe it had already covered the boat, but he could see his seat! He turned through three-hundred and sixty degrees and then a few more, scanning, scrutinising and praying, and it still wasn't there.

Destroyed and distraught he sat on the one thing that was there and cried in despair.

'Let's look at this logically.' he said out loud and to no-one in particular. 'I'm the man who travelled back in time to see Grace in nineteen-forty-four in her hour of need. I'm the man who thought he was speaking to a dragon, disguised as a boat, that isn't there anymore. It may never have been there, so what do I make of that? I'm also the man who has levered thoughts straight out of other peoples minds. I'm fucking David Blaine!'

'Back to number one... why did I go back in time? To help a distressed young girl grieving for her father? Okay, number two... was I actually speaking to myself the whole time? Maybe I just put the boat there from my own imagination, sort of a softener to reason with what was happening? Moving onto number three... Can I read minds? And if I can, why and for what reason? Number four... I'm not David Blaine! Woo Hoo! One down three to go!'

Miles felt something moving from under the wet leg of his torn trousers, he rolled up the left trouser-leg and blood trickled freely from an open wound. He covered it with a hand and the blood seeped through his fingers, onto the back of his hand to drip and mingle with the gravel, sand and seaweed. 'No pain!' He closed his eyes and considered those two words carefully. 'No pain.'

Grace was in pain the day he met her for the first time, the pain of grief, he'd tried his utmost to help and failed. Why had he failed? Because Grace was removed from his counsel before she understood what he was trying to tell her. But Grace was too young to understand, he'd needed more time with her. Mhairi too, she'd been in pain, both physical and mental. He wanted to help her, to give her something, a gift if you like, to make Mhairi's life just a little more special. And Julic, she missed Skip as much as he did, maybe even more so. His own grief was fortified by frustration so he'd run to this place... and it had begun. He wished he could have gone back in time to that moment when he had run from Julie, he'd change everything.

'So, if I accept that it's always been me, as Grace was keen to point out, what am I?'

'I'm the dragon, I'm Death, I'm the beithir and... I'm Miles!'

'So where has this power come from? Come on, Miles there aren't many things to choose from! God?

Mmm, I don't think so, he'd have chosen a believer to do his good work. The dragon or the beithir?'

Miles thought of what he'd been told, the beithir was one of the fuathan, a sort of dragon or serpent, but in the main, it was a water spirit. Perhaps a spirit had entered his body! When though? When he was inadequately scattering the ashes of Skip? Skip?

'There's no way it could be Skip, surely it can't be that simple, the spirit of a dead dog... No! Scrub that... the spirit of my best friend, Skip.'

'Okay I'm getting nowhere with the creation of what I have become. I'll accept that I can do these things, preferring the last explanation as to where this gift has come from. So, why?' Miles looked down at the blood pooling at his feet and pulled his trouser-leg up further to explore the new wound. He circled a finger lightly around the large patch of missing skin, tightening the circular motion into an inwards spiral and expecting any second to grimace from the pain as his finger scraped across exposed nerve endings. The pain didn't come. He forced himself to poke and prod at the ripped flesh, and still there was no pain. 'What the hell!' Snatching his trouser-leg back down to cover the mess he'd made of his shin he tried to remember the last time he'd felt actual pain.

The handshake with Mr MacLeod, well that was just a firm handshake. It hadn't really hurt, it had just stopped the flow of his blood for a moment and made his fingers go numb. The first time he was on the beach, the time he'd gone a-sprawling trying to run from the voice in his head. Really, it hadn't hurt, probably adrenalin, he'd played on it at the time, trying to attract any sympathy vote out of Julie. He'd even been asked, on next meeting the dragon, how his hands were, he hadn't considered it relevant until now. But it wasn't the dragon, was it? It had just been Miles!

Something gnawed at his brain, something Mhairi had said and it had just come back to him. 'She doesn't want you to know yet!'

'Is it about the lack of feeling pain?' he asked

'No, it's worse than that.' he replied to himself, and felt surprised that he was now answering his own questions with that same voice he'd heard and almost recognised, his own.

'What's worse than not feeling any pain?'

'Feeling too much or not feeling anything!'

Miles didn't ask any more questions for a few minutes, he mulled over the last sentence not wishing to know more. He didn't speak until he formulated the questions *he* wanted the answers to and in an order, he felt, that *he* could handle those answers. In the end there was only the one question though. 'What don't you want me to know?'

'You're dying, Miles. You have been from the moment I found you.'

'But I feel so- well, I'm not ill and I'm not in pain.'

'If I release you, Miles, you will be in considerable pain!' As if to prove the fact, Miles felt a portion of something deep inside slowly ebb from his body, to be replaced by a tightening of his chest that strangled his willingness to breathe. The pain eased and once again he was re-united with his guest.

'So what are you?' he managed to ask himself, once the pain had receeded.

'I'm the beithir and the dragon, I've been death and yes, I am one of the so-called Fuathan. I *am* a water spirit! I'm you!'

'And you found me where?'

Images of the bridge across the River Coe, on the day he scattered Skip's ashes, invaded his mind. He could feel the air, the dampness. The cold parapet of the bridge under his fingertips as he leant over it, how he was deeply engrossed in his own thoughts of Skip. Every aspect, like it was still happening now. He tried to shut the pictures and the feelings down but everything played out, just like it had when he'd met Grace. The whole story, from that singular moment to now. When it was over he opened his eyes. Only moments had passed.

'So what has happened to me?'

'I have given you the gift of a pain free end to your life. You are a water spirit now!'

'That's it! I die pain free and that's it! Pain free with a part of me being a water spirit!'

'Shut up and listen! You have choices to make, there are things you have done that are incomplete, they need completing. Now is your time act. Your last time!'

Miles told himself everything he needed to know and more besides and before he was finished he had started walking back towards the campsite, away from the beach, and towards his awaiting friends. As he got to the road Phillip was there, watching his approach; Phillip's car parked half on the road and half on the pavement a little way further up the road. Phillip didn't comment on Miles's lack of footwear or lack of coat, nor did he mention the ripped trousers or the bloody wound that the torn fabric barely concealed. He just placed his arm about Miles's waist and helped him to the car in total silence. Miles accepted the help without question, glad that he wasn't being quizzed or being called an idiot. But more, he was thankful that it was Phillip that had been sent to hunt him down and return him to the fold. He knew it would be Phillip. Mhairi would have called him, all three women would have told him where to go. The only place Miles could, and would, go.

The air about him seemed to still and he felt like he was disappearing into it. He certainly wanted to. He looked at the four dumb-struck faces staring back at him, feeling like he should run from them again, but his legs refused to obey like he was glued to the seat. He withdrew into his own thoughts and shut the doors to all of them for a while. Vaguely, he could hear them talking away. To him, and about him, but he didn't want to become involved, not yet, it was safer if he didn't. Everything he heard seemed to wash over him as if he were completely invisible and that was just what he wanted, total withdrawal.

Through the mist that he felt surrounded him, he looked down at Skye, asleep and unknowing upon the rug, and wished he were her, oblivious to all that had happened and all that would happen. Curled up contentedly and ready to accept her new life. He thought about the smiling optimism of Phillip, faced with an uncertain future he still remained a jovial gentleman, gallant and a person that, Miles found, he admired immensely. A dull ache in his chest, hardly perceptible, made itself known, and he felt an urgency to join the land of the living for a while longer.

He looked to Grace, he looked inside her, carefully, tentatively, trying not to disturb her. She knew he was there and smiled at him. There was something so beautiful about that smile and Miles saw the girl that was, all of those years ago, the vitality was still there, that vital spark.

Mhairi next, Mhairi who was helping Julie to tend to his injuries. No need this time to feign pain, he was never going to get any more brownie points that way. Mhairi started at his subtle exploration of her mind, considering trying to block the tranquil foray, ultimately deciding to allow it in, in the end. She looked up into his eyes and he saw the tears there that streamed like there was no tomorrow, and Mhairi new that there wouldn't be a tomorrow, not like this. She tried to look away but something forced her eyes back to his. Then through it all, she smiled.

Julie, the love of his life, stood up and moved away from him, her face full of concern. Miles called her back softly and she turned and reached out a hand to him. Miles held it clamping and burying it in both of his hands. He never wanted to let it go again. But things were happening which were beyond his control and he only had minutes now. Julie saw, she couldn't say what she saw but it was there. She called his name, trying to shake him gently back into reality. Miles saw her face, like through a veil. 'I love you, always have, and always will.' he whispered in his mind and she heard him. 'Skye is for you!'

Activity in the motorhome accelerated, a flurry of faces and movement, but everything seemed to be moving in slow motion, taking eons to unfold. Mhairi was speaking urgently into her mobile phone. Grace reached out her hand to take his. 'I'm so sorry Grace, I couldn't save you then.' He watched as she mouthed some words in reply.

'Thank you, Miles, for trying to help me. It was always you and you did help. Miles?' 'Miles?' Grace thought without words and she knew Miles had heard.

'Phillip's going to be there for you now!'

Mhairi, tears coursing her cheeks, mentioned that an ambulance was on its way. Miles spoke to her through the all-encompassing fog. 'I'm sorry, Mhairi!'

'There's nothing to be sorry for, I met you, didn't I? And that's been enough for me.' Mhairi spoke quietly. Julie couldn't work out what Mhairi had heard to warrant such a reply.

Julie sat down next to him and put an arm around his neck, he could feel the warmth from her arm and felt her pull him closer,. 'I love you, I love you.' and she kept saying it, rocking him gently against her body and never letting go.

With resignation came complete revelation, he knew everything he needed to know, it had always been him and all he had wanted to do was to help people. He didn't know where it had come from, this samaritan thing, this water spirit thing, but he'd needed to do it. Everybody needs to do it! He'd tried so hard to help Grace and had believed he had failed, but now things would turn out okay, he was sure of that, she'd got Phillip now! Mhairi had come out of her shell, he'd tried to help her too, to come to terms with her burns, she'd be alright, she had Julie as a good friend now!

And he knew why he had to get Skye, it was never for him, it was a gift for Julie. It didn't make him feel any better about leaving her, but it went some of the way, he supposed. 'Skye's yours, Julie.' he thought again. And she knew.

Miles wanted desperately to say 'I'll be back' but it didn't seem appropriate and he knew it would come out flat and wrong, not Arnie.

Miles was more water spirit than Miles now, instead he stared up into Julie's watery eyes and, with every ounce of love left inside him, he pushed the seeds of an idea out towards her. Miles knew it would be a while before the idea flowered, but he hoped it would help her in the future. For one week he'd been blessed with a power to do something extraordinary. And this was the end of that week.

Slowly, so slowly the insides of the van disappeared entirely from his vision, he felt nothing, his soul united with the timeless spirit that had looked after him in his last week of life. He still heard Julie's words, and they made everything seem right.

Miles lay on the floor of the motorhome, Julie cradling his head, holding it tilted back and looking into his eyes, repeating her mantra to him, 'I love you! Please, Miles? I love you.' She rocked backwards and forwards in time.

Mhairi, driven by a new found strength, refused to give up on Miles and continued to perform Cardiopulmonary Resuscitation. After ten minutes her arms ached and sweat rolled from her forehead to join her tears and her eyes stung. She never stopped. Twenty minutes passed by and she still kept up the rhythm, thirty compressions, two breaths, thirty compressions, two breaths. Her arms were burning with the effort, screaming at her to relent, to give in, but she dared not stop. Only when the ambulance arrived did she condescend, reluctantly, to relinquish her charge, and she crawled away and slumped to the floor with her back against the door to the shower, watching Julie rocking backwards and forwards, Miles's head in her lap.

Phillip had taken Grace outside and the paramedics tried to prise Julie apart from Miles.

'Just bloody leave them be for a while!' Mhairi screamed. 'It's over!'

Chapter 19

The old Morris Minor mostly flew down the motorway with the wind pushing at the back doors in assistance. Empty now of Phillip's collection of what was important to him, the car summited the hills with ease and coasted down the other side maintaining a solid sixty rising to seventy miles-per-hour on the descents. Mhairi drove and Julie sat at her side in the passenger seat. It took twelve hours to get from Glencoe to Woodbridge in Suffolk, to finally arrive at Julie and Miles's old home.

Phillip had made all of the arrangements, he'd loaned them his pride and joy, but he couldn't accompany them, much as he wanted to. Grace didn't feel able to make the journey and Phillip felt that his place was now with Grace. He believed that Miles would understand, not that Miles was there to argue the point. Neither Julie nor Mhairi pushed it any further and they made the trip together, to say a farewell to Miles in his home town.

A very private funeral and cremation occurred two weeks after they had set off, attended by Miles's workmates and a few close friends, but none closer than Mhairi had become. Mhairi sorted through everything that needed doing and all the while, keeping a close eye on Julie and being there for her when things seemed hopeless. The times when Julie just wanted to curl up and die too. And they happened often. But that was not allowed to happen.

The post mortem results provided few answers. Sudden arrhythmic death syndrome, the acronym of it appeared on the death certificate. It didn't say how, or why, he had died of it. One of the doctors had mentioned Brugada Syndrome, an inherited condition more prevalent in people with East Asian connections, indeed, Miles's own mother was from Hong Kong and it fitted with the assumption, but it was too late to prove it had been that. An assumption it remained. So SADS was what was written upon the death certificate.

On the night before they left back towards Glencoe, one month after they had arrived in the town of Woodbridge, they sat on the floor in the empty living room and opened a bottle of wine. Two china mugs today, the cut crystal glasses had been packed away ready for a journey. They raised their mugs in a toast to Miles, like they had every night that they'd been there, and every night there had been fewer and fewer items of furniture to dispose of or to get ready for relocation.

Mhairi pointed at a point above the fireplace and said. 'That picture would have looked nice there.'

'What picture?'

'The one I was going to give you, so you'd never forget about me.'

Julie looked at the bare wall. 'You were never going to give me that picture.' she said.

'It was mine to give and I couldn't think of a better person to give it to.'

'But it was hours and hours of work, you might have sold it!'

'It's not all about the money though, is it?' Julie had heard it had been said before, Mr MacLeod!

'I suppose it isn't.' The two mugs clunked hollowly together.

'Mr MacLeod saw that too, when he gave Skye to Miles,' Mhairi said. 'he would rather give Skye away to a good home than take a million pounds for her. I hope she's okay.'

Skye was back at Mr MacLeod's, awaiting Julie's return, she'd not even spent one night with her new owners, oh! owner now! And Julie wondered how she was getting on.

'About Skye?' she asked. 'How did Miles know?'

Mhairi looked thoughtful for a few moments before attempting to answer. 'I think he was able to do something rather special. He was able to step away from his own self and explore other people's minds.'

'But how?'

'I don't know how, but he managed it. Maybe it was because he was unwell.'

'What about Grace?'

'That's even harder to understand, he'd only heard of her through a story, and her name never came up. He sought her out somehow, caused *her* to find him. How the hell he visited her all those years ago, I have no idea. Perhaps the dragon was real after all, maybe the dragon became a part of Miles in the end.'

'So what do you think happened when Miles could no longer talk to the dragon?'

'I think whatever needed doing had been done by then, the dragon's work here was finished.'

'Miles didn't have any symptoms of a heart problem, he never had any pain, he just went so quickly.'

'Perhaps the dragon helped there too.' said Mhairi.

'Maybe!' Julie started to cry again and Mhairi put her arm around her and held on to her until she stopped.

They took two days to get back to Glencoe, the car was a lot fuller now and a lot slower. Julie remembered how Miles had always said, it was slower going to Scotland because it was all up hill, but Julie didn't agree with that. Julie's idea that the journey up was always longer was because of the expectancy, akin to waiting for Christmas day to arrive as a child. And when it arrived, time just flew by again. The journey back home would always be shorter because of the return to mundanity.

At just after eleven in the morning after driving through the night, they pulled the car up outside Mhairi's house, Mr MacLeod saw them arrive and came out to meet them with Skye. He passed the lead to Julie and asked. 'All sorted?' She nodded her reply, he gave her a short hug then he nodded back with a brusque understanding and turned and walked back to his own house leaving Julie with the dog. Julie led Skye up to her new temporary home, three doors away from her old home.

When the money came through for the property in Woodbridge she'd get somewhere of her own, local. She wouldn't be returning to Woodbridge anytime soon though. Miles, it seems, had seen to that.

The next day, based on an understanding made before they had left for Woodbridge, Mhairi telephoned Phillip and arranged for them to all meet up at the Clachaig.

Outside the sun shone, it was warm enough to dispense with coats and not a cloud marred the sky.

Julie wore the rucksack first, she'd wear it until it became somewhat lighter, a time that would herald a return to the Inn. Skye ran ahead on the footpath through the woods, turning often to ensure that Julie was still following. At each road crossing they had to make on their way up the glen, Skye came to a halt and awaited their arrival, for Julie to see her safely across to the footpath on the opposite side before she bounded off again. Just before the Clachaig, she accepted being leashed and walked to heel into the car park.

Grace and Phillip were already outside the Inn waiting for them, they hugged Julie and Mhairi in turn and exchanged pleasantries, then they followed, falling into step behind Mhairi and Julie. Walking away from the Inn and towards the little bridge over the River Coe.

Instead of standing at the bridge parapet, Mhairi led them down the steep slope to the water's edge and out onto a sizable grassy area with a large rock that dipped its toes into the river. Phillip helped Grace down to join them.

'We do this properly!' Phillip announced with authority and opened his own rucksack to retrieve five cut crystal glasses and a bottle of twenty-five year old Bunnahabhain. He broke the seal and poured five whisky's, placing them carefully onto a rock nearby, in readiness.

Mhairi helped Julie from the rucksack she carried, and pulled from it the urn. She prised off the lid and passed it to Julie standing right at the very limits of the large rock. Julie poured, allowing the ash to trickle slowly upon the surface of the fast moving water. Behind her, Mhairi, Grace and Phillip watched on in silence, even Skye seemed to realise the importance of the occasion and sat still at Mhairi's feet, looking on and taking it all in.

When the ash ceased to flow, Julie stepped back away from the edge, watching the last speckles of grey and white drift off downstream and the clouds of lighter material settle onto the water to be carried away. Phillip passed the glasses around. Wordlessly, and without a prompt, four of the glasses were raised in a silent toast, the sunlight shone through the whisky and cast a soft glow upon the hands that held each glass. The company sipped at their drinks, embroiled, each alone, in their own thoughts and recollections of Miles.

As each glass emptied, one remained and it was Grace who picked it up. She walked down to the edge of the river and poured it ceremoniously into the stream, to blend with the river and chase the ashes onwards towards the sea and Skip. Softly and deliberately, she spoke in Gaelic.

Julie looked to Mhairi for a translation. 'What did Grace say?' she asked quietly.

'It was something like, May god give you a drink from the well that never runs dry.' she paused. 'He'd have liked that.' Mhairi turned away to hide her tears.

Julie bit her lip, hard and said. 'Come on now, lets go to the pub and get pissed! Miles would have liked that too!' She turned her back and led the way, hiding a torrent of silent tears.

Firmly settled into the alcove that they had used on their previous visit, the drinks flowed and nobody lacked for liquid sustenance or conversation. Tongues loosened and Grace suddenly and starkly made an announcement in the flow of another generalised, meandering, moment. It stopped dead the train of all of their thoughts.

'Phillip doesn't have a tumour anymore!'

The silence that followed seemed to last for minutes, it seemed that all sound in the bar was swallowed. Phillip sheepishly broke the consuming silence. 'It's true, I don't know how, but the tumour has- well it's not shrunk, it hasn't grown, it's just- gone.'

'But you said it was inoperable, that you were on your final world tour!' Mhairi exclaimed.

'I know. But I *will* get the tumour back, if it will please you, Mhairi.'

Mhairi stood up from her perch on the bench seat and rounded the table heading for Phillip, she squeezed her small frame between the table and the opposite bench seat and plonked her backside down upon Phillip's lap, finally wrapping her arms about his shoulders.

'You'd better fucking not.' she whispered into his ear and kissed him.

'Any more amazing news?' asked Julie.

'Well, just this little bit of news. If you'll excuse me for a while Mhairi.' Phillip eased Mhairi up and away from him before fumbling about in his jacket pocket and turning to face Grace. 'Will you do me the honour of being my-'

'Oh stop it you fool, you know I said yes the first time you asked me.'

'Ahhh, but this time I've got the ring to make it official.'

Phillip opened the small ring case and retrieved the engagement band from within before placing it lovingly on Grace's finger. The sapphire and diamond ring was huge in comparison to her dainty fingers but the velvety-blue main stone sat perfectly, surrounded by smaller diamonds, and perfect for Grace. Julie looked at Grace's facial features then back towards the finger on the hand that bore the ring. Had she been away so long as to forget how smooth Grace's complexion was? Grace was surely ageing in the wrong direction. As Julie once again looked at Grace's face, she saw how happy and content Grace had become. 'It must be down to Phillip.' she thought.

Both Julie and Mhairi, for a while, were open-mouthed and totally at a loss for words until the flood gates finally opened up and questions poured from them both.

'When did all this happen? Let's see the ring again? Why didn't you tell us earlier? You could have phoned! When's the happy day?'

'Let me stop you there!' said Grace. 'There isn't going to be a wedding.'

'But there has to be!' complained Mhairi.

'We are engaged, and that is that, it's all we want and it is *our* commitment to each other.'

'But why not just go that little bit further?' asked Julie, still mesmerised by Grace's flawless skin.

'Because this is what makes *us* happy. This is the start of our happy days, to commit our lives to each other, engaged with each other, for as long as we have.' Phillip leant across and kissed Grace. 'Now I know we have had a sad start to the day,' Grace pushed Phillip

235

aside and stared directly into Julie's eyes. 'but I have it on good authority that this is what Miles intended for us.'

Julie almost got to ask, 'Why?' But Grace had fixed her with a gaze that spoke, 'Not now! Later!'

'Now an engagement party seems to be a good idea...' said Phillip,

After many questions and quite a few answers, quite a few toasts, undoubtably one too many times, where glasses started to take on the mystical power where they could never be emptied, the day was drawing to a close, from an imbibing point of view. Thoughts turned to reaching Mhairi's house and possibly a coffee or four. Phillip approached the bar and spoke to one of the staff to arrange for a taxi to take them back down the glen.

At Mhairi's house, they all sat around in the lounge. 'Can I see what you've been working on in your studio?' Phillip asked at the slightest of signals from Grace. Julie saw it, that minute nod of her head in his direction and Phillip reacting like a trained puppy.

Julie smiled at Grace. 'You've got him trained well!'

'There's a way to go yet, but he's getting it.' Grace replied. 'You've been staring at me all day, haven't you? Every chance you get, staring. And you've noticed something that's- not as it should be, haven't you?'

'I'm sorry,' Julie said awkwardly.

'Nothing to be sorry for. You noticed, that's that. What have you seen? You can be open and honest, it won't offend me.'

'It's just that-' Julie found some resolve. 'the first time we saw you, you looked so frail, you looked ninety.'

'And now?'

'And now you don't look anywhere near ninety years old!' Grace smiled and prompted for more.

'So what age am I now?'

'A bloody good looking sixty-something.' Julie answered and Grace feigned hurt.

'Phillip says fifty if I'm a day!' she laughed as Julies face had taken on an expression of worry of an offence perceived by Grace.

'And what about Phillip?' Julie asked. 'No-one recovers from an inoperable brain tumour! Especially when they've only been given months to live, if that!'

'Well Phillip disproves that, doesn't he?'

'Grace, what is going on?' Julie asked in exasperation.

Grace knew that now was the time to stop messing with Julie, but she was unsure how what she had to say would be taken. 'I think it's a gift, Julie.'

'Who from? Only god can give away gifts like those the two of you have!'

'It's not from god, it's definitely not from him.'

'So who then?'

'Would you like to hazard a guess?'

'I can't. Please just tell me.'

'Please, just listen, Julie. Please don't say anything until I have completely finished. I'm going to tell you what I think has happened and it may not be to your liking what I have to say, but say it I must.'

'Okay.' Julie sat back in her armchair and closed her eyes. As ready as she could be, to hear what Grace had to say.

Grace took a deep breath before starting.

'When I was a child I saw a man on the beach, the day I learned that my father had been killed in France. I assumed it was Death, because that's who I called out for when all I wanted to do was die. It wasn't Death. Even though he tried to tell me he wasn't Death, I didn't believe him and persisted in my childish appraisal of him. The man I saw that day was Miles! The man I continued to see on all of my other visits to that beach, was Miles. I don't know how, but I think I know why and I'll come back to that in a while.

'Miles knew, that what happened, as a consequence of him being there, didn't go quite the way he wanted it to. I ended up being whisked away to Glasgow and he couldn't find me anymore to put things right. Many years later, when I eventually became known again to Miles, he tried to contact me through my dreams, but I wasn't having any of it, remembering what happened last time. The last dream I had though, had real people in it. Yourself, Skip and Miles. Real people in a real place, harmless and intriguing. The next day I came to see whether any of it was real. On that day I wasn't being guided towards the beach and Death, I was discreetly checking out the possibility that there were actual people that I could speak to, not spectres or phantoms. And I recognised Miles. Not just from the dream, but because it was Miles I had spoken with, all of those years ago. You pretty much know the rest but what you don't know is that on that last day Miles spoke to me. He spoke to Mhairi too I think, and to you, but I'm not sure you heard. He spoke with his mind, not vocally, before you tell me you know.'

'Miles was given a gift, a gift from something that is-thought to be mythological, a gift from a fuath.' Julie smiled her recognition of the word. 'Well, you've obviously heard of the fuathan then.' Grace continued. 'They're water spirits and that is what Miles is too.'

'IS!' Julie couldn't help it. 'Is?'

'Miles had a pain free death, part of the gift. And in return Miles has been given the chance to bestow gifts of his own as one of the fuathan. I think everything that's happening now is down to Miles, Phillip and I have had our gifts. It's to be yours and Mhairi's turn next. Well, that's it.

Julie thought about what Grace had said for a few moments before asking. 'I thought the fuath were malevolent?'

'I thought they were mythological, shows what we know eh?'

Plockton village hall was available for the whole week and Julie had secured a showing of Mhairi's paintings, without having to share the wall space with fellow artists; some little way to pay her back for all of the hours that Mhairi had spent looking out for her. Now, Julie had her own house that she shared with Skye and a job she loved, working with an artist; more, working with a good friend.

Advertising literature had been commissioned for the event and even the local radio station was on the case with an interview, live on air; Julie had seen to that too. Mhairi had dusted off enough works to fill every inch of available space with her paintings, each original piece had it's own price tag, but if that was too steep then you could buy a framed, or unframed, print to be able to appreciate her art in the comfort of your own home at a more affordable price.

Now, Julie and Mhairi sat at a small table in the middle of the room whilst outside, the summers sun encouraged a stream of gallery visitors. While they watched the constant flow of viewers and buyers, they both knew that the artworks were definitely selling and the week long excursion had been more than worthwhile.

Occasionally Skye looked up from a crude bed beneath the table to ascertain whether it was walk-time or pub-time yet.

As another credit card transaction needed to be made, one or other of them would show the purchaser into the hall where the credit card machine was kept, if it was cash- a small blue strong-box was opened to take the notes and provide the change. Mhairi signed her name and wrote simple explanations of the pieces as they sold, whatever the customer wanted, Mhairi was there to help. Julie placed yellow labels on the original pieces that had sold, with a number giving reference to the name and address where the painting would be going after the showing was over. Skye took it all in then lowered her head to rest it upon her paws again.

Upon the farthest wall, centrally placed, the biggest of the pieces hung, surrounded by smaller frames that bore a resemblance to the larger item, but not the image. The wall wore a sign above the paintings that proclaimed them 'The Beithir Collection', each had a yellow sticker in the corner of their frames, all but one had a reference number, the largest and darkest of the images.

Julie had got used to seeing Mhairi's rendition of Miles, dressed in waterproofs, wet and glimmering with the droplets of water that beaded on his coat and leggings, she'd even been there when it was painted. That didn't mean she liked it, somehow it appeared quite hollow, it hadn't really captured the essence of Miles in life. Even though Miles's face shone out from under the black hood, watching from every angle and his clothing looked like it contained a million stars, set against the rugged backdrop of the beach and the sky held an aurora, dark but not black, colourful but not bright, layers of deep paint hinting at the hues of the aurora but never quite giving the whole story away. She hated it.

It was a quarter to closing time and a customer approached Mhairi after having stood in the room, and before the painting, for a lot longer than was necessary. A young man wearing clothing that proclaimed he had arrived by yacht, probably moored out in the bay. Bright yellow oilies, Dubarry boots, and wearing a blue cap that bore the insignia of the Lelystad Yacht Haven, crowned his head.

He spoke with a Dutch accent, but with impeccable English. 'Can I ask about that piece?' he pointed back at the main painting on the wall. Mhairi and Julie looked towards the painting.

'What would you like to know?' asked Mhairi appraising the man. Julie watched on, accepting begrudgingly that the painting was already hers. Hopeful that an offer that couldn't be refused were to be made in the next few minutes

'Did you paint that?'

'Yes, but it's already sold I'm afraid.'

'I don't want to buy it, it's just that- something weird is happening with it.'

She stopped undressing the man with her eyes and looked at the handsome man in surprise. Standing up quickly to follow him. 'What's wrong with it?'

'It's the paint, I think something's been spilled over it.'

Mhairi moved quickly towards the painting, Julie fell in behind her and Skye wasn't too far behind Julie. The man led the way and stopped before the painting. 'Look!' he said, and pointed towards the centre of the canvas. They all looked to where he was pointing.

In the very centre of the piece, the paint had taken on a new life of its own, the paint seemed to swirl and rotate slowly. New colours appeared and disappeared as an impossible rotation started to spread from that part of the painting that was actually the hooded head of Miles. Suddenly, the swirling stopped and the paint, liquid and pliant, fanned out from the centre quickly, like a huge globule of multi-hued, shiny, brilliant acrylic had been dropped upon a dark, spinning, horizontal surface from a great height, it spattered outwards towards the four corners and solidified. None of the underlying image was disturbed, it was still all there, but a more vivid, urgent, light had melded into the darkness surrounding the image of Miles. The painting now radiated an aura that hadn't been there before, not on the original paint, but within it. As they watched the darkest layers of paint that remained started to glow like burning coals, ruby red, shimmering in and out of focus like a myriad points of fire had been embedded into the canvas and had now erupted to life.

Julie gasped as she perceived an image of Skip, blended into view within the paint to join Miles. Suddenly life had entered into the dark image that, in her mind, initially, was dour and drab.

The man looked at Mhairi. 'Is that meant to happen?' he asked, sounding out of breath.

'I think it is.' Julie answered on Mhairi's behalf.

'Very good!' he said. 'I didn't expect that. Very good, excellent, in fact.' He backed away from the painting, hoping to see more, but there was no more to see in his eyes. Mhairi ushered him away from the painting, doing her best to explain how she had incorporated Led's into the piece and how she would have to switch them off now as it was closing time. He walked reluctantly away, content with her explanation, but not content that he was being parted from the artist who had painted it. He resolved to track her down.

Jos, had indeed sailed into Plockton that morning, he'd anchored his yacht in the bay and wandered about the village leaving his crew to do their own things. Dining in the Plockton hotel with it's weird black and white stone frontage, he had noticed Mhairi, out to get lunch herself, and- Mhairi was the most beautiful woman he'd ever laid eyes upon. The scars, he'd noticed, beneath the inked sleeves, didn't matter a jot. Mhairi was definitely the most beautiful woman he'd ever seen and he would find a way to tell her.

Once the man was heading back down the road in the direction of the pub, Mhairi considering his physique as he walked, she carefully shut the door behind him and threw one of the bolts across to lock it temporarily before entering the hall once again.

Mhairi and Julie stood for a long time watching the painting with its twists and turns, evolving and devolving, eventually, they sat on the floor before it, watching it evaporate and reform before their eyes as a story in acrylic performed parts of a life so missed. The voice spoke quietly through the silence of the room, a voice that was there but hidden inside, and Mhairi heard it and understood, she looked at Julie, nudged her and caught her attention, drawing it way from the painting for a brief moment.

'He's asking whether you are ready for what comes next?' Mhairi asked. Julie looked at her face and saw that she was crying, waves of tears coursed her cheeks but she looked happy.

Julie nodded and did not know what to expect, she'd been here before and when she had been asked whether she wanted to speak with the dragon, she had declined. Now, the option of yes or no did not seem to apply. It was the lesser of two-. The easiest decision in the world. Julie, immediately, was saturated with that of the voice. The voice of a woman but the voice of- Death, Dragon and Beithir, fuath. Miles

Mhairi left the hall leaving Julie with Skye and Miles. She was sure there would be someone worth looking out for in the pub.

Julie sat and talked without a sound, she closed her eyes, she cried, she smiled, she laughed. It had been so long since she'd laughed.

Skye just wondered what all the fuss was about, she'd heard it all before, from Skip.

Epilogue

Today,

Ellis Hawes wandered away from his home and onto the path that followed the river as it wound its way downwards towards the sea. Twenty-three years old and still unable to speak, Ellis lived, trapped, in a world of his own. Not that it bothered him one iota. People spoke about autism and the autism spectrum as if it were a bad thing, but to Ellis, he'd known nothing else, it was just the way it was. He never questioned being different, he didn't care for spectrums, Ellis was Ellis, and that was that.

The river Deben had always been on his doorstep and he'd always lived in the same house in a village called Melton, just on the outskirts of a small town called Woodbridge. He was a fine figure of a man, quite muscular from his work helping his dad at one of the boatyards in the town. A shock of brown hair with a natural wave across his brow, tanned, and mesmerisingly blue eyes. Under other circumstances, certainly a catch with the women, but most women tended to give him a wide berth as soon as he opened his mouth. It didn't phase him, nothing did, he'd learnt in the past that getting frustrated by the people around him didn't do any good, he plodded through life now. Happy.

Working in a boat yard came about as seamlessly as everything in his life had, with total acceptance.

He moved fluidly from one scenario to the next, never questioning why he did one thing instead of another. His work there was exemplary, he handled wood for the main part, cutting it, shaping it, joining it. To the ends of building or the repairing of wooden boats. He enjoyed spending hours attending to one intricately shaped piece and grafting it into place; working out the angles and invisible joints between two such pieces, ensuring that they would last and be as pleasing to look at in the years to come as they were now. Other boat builders in the yard marvelled at his skill and wondered how he had learnt it, but to Ellis, it was just what he did, he didn't know why he was so good at it or how he'd learnt it and he didn't care.

After work he often walked back home along the river footpath and he knew every inch of the walk. Today was Saturday though, and he didn't have to work, his plan was just to amble along in the general direction of the town, maybe see what wildlife was around upon the saltings and amble back in time for lunch.

When Ellis had first started his roaming's away from home, his mother or father had followed him to make sure he was alright. To begin with they'd made no attempt to keep their following a secret, but as time passed by, they decided to almost hide from him. To give him some freedom. He knew one of them would be there, behind him, somewhere at a distance. Today he looked behind at the path he'd trodden and didn't see anyone scurrying for cover, covertly trailing him.

He smiled to himself and hummed inanely. To an outsider, to everyone really, that could here his inane tune as he continued his march foreward, it would be just that, inane. To Ellis, it concentrated his mind, things got put into perspective when he hummed. He hummed, loudly.

The sun shone brightly, Spring was in the air and everything was coming back to life after months of dormancy. He walked the footpath through one boatyard and into the next. He passed by the boats on the hard and the moored and tethered yachts and motorboats on the water. Passing by the floating homes, the house boats, he stopped for a moment to gaze upon the grey hulk of a ship, now re-utilised as a cafe. The smell of frying bacon carried on the air taunted and caught up with him. He so wanted to walk up the ramp to board the vessel and partake of a bacon butty, but he felt that by that action alone, he would be revealed as something- undesirable. Just ordering the bacon sandwich would be an ordeal, let alone sitting there to eat it. He didn't need that hassle.

He continued along the river wall passing one of the sluices that drained the land of frequent flood water. At the corner where the larger house boats were moored he was struck by a picture he hadn't seen before. Out in the mud, twenty feet from the flood-wall, lay the wreck of an old wooden boat, mostly submerged and stripped of anything of worth. The topsides were incomplete, exposing the stringers that strengthened the vessel. The deck was just a memory, Ellis could make out the shelves that would have supported the decking. A part of the rudder hung onto the stern of the boat like a limpet and the rotten tiller struck for the sky at a rakish angle.

Ellis couldn't remember seeing the wreck there before, he assumed it was because it may have only recently been revealed, maybe the mud had been washed away, mud that had fully enveloped it at one time. The tides sometimes brought to light its buried secrets in such a way, usually after a storm or a surge tide. He thought back over the recent weather and tidal heights and couldn't place an irregularity there that might cause such a revelation.

Hoisting himself up to sit upon the sun-warmed steel flood-barrier atop the wall that separated the footpath from the tidal river, he gazed at the remains and tried to figure out, in his head, what sort of vessel she had been. She wasn't deep enough to be a Thames barge, and she wasn't Dutch built, the low deck level reminded him of a Norfolk Wherry. Looking for signs of the mast position, he located strengthened beams well forward, attached to the hull and rising upwards to support the diminished deck, taking that into account he could picture the mast in place and the boat was slowly rebuilt in his mind's eye. 'What the hell was a Norfolk Wherry doing in the river Deben?' He imagined the question, a question he was unable to deliver verbally. He pictured the complete boat with its shallow draft and huge sail area, trying to make the treacherous entrance to the river from the sea. Wherry's were a sedate craft, designed to sail the rivers and broads, not the sea. Undoubtably, a few had ventured out, but they would have been unwieldy in any decent coastal breeze. So how had this one got here?

Ellis's stomach rumbled and he wished he had taken breakfast that morning, he pictured the bacon sandwich he could have had if only he were able to have asked for it. Frustration was something he'd lived with the whole of his life, never being able to get what he wanted when he wanted it. As a child he worked with flash-cards, and as he progressed through school he carried them on his person, to show someone, if the need arose, exactly what he wanted. Adults didn't carry flash-cards and Ellis wanted to fit in with his peers, so now he didn't carry flash-cards either.

A bloody bacon sandwich, so simple to ask for, for anyone else, but so beyond Ellis's means. He clawed at his face and wailed nasally, as was his way when faced with an unobtainable target, holding his head in his hands, curling and straightening his fingers, dragging his nails up and down his temples, scratching deep into his skin to allow the feeling of pain to overtake his feeling of hopelessness.

Somebody spoke, making him jump, he looked around to find the source of the voice but no-one was there.

'Ellis?'

The sound came from everywhere, more like an invasion into his brain. Ellis put his fingers into his ears to try and block it out, even muffle the acuteness of the blare he heard. Quieter now, the voice called his name again. 'Ellis?'

Ellis knew that no-one was around, there wasn't a person alive that could creep up on him to deliver such a vocal punch. He removed his fingers from his ears and lowered his hands away from his face. 'Ellis?'

'What?' he thought and hummed his own audible version of the intended question.

'Please don't claw at your face again, Ellis!' said the voice. 'and please don't get upset, I can understand everything you want me to!'

Ellis wanted to know who could speak to him in such a way, he wasn't unnerved by the sudden intrusion into his head, it didn't phase him that there was no physical being delivering the voice, Ellis accepted it much in the same way he had to accept everything else. He lowered his left hand and started to shake it, as was his way. He wanted to ask questions and he imagined them. And for the first time, when he pictured his question, he perceived an answer, and it all made perfect sense to him.

The End

CPSIA information can be obtained
at www.ICGtesting.com
Printed in the USA
LVHW091918110222
710698LV00004B/51

9 781839 759307